CAJUN IS HIT!

As Cajun Lee reached for his Colt, a rifle slug tore through his left side, tugging him down. He hit the dirt with his right hand empty. The gun had flipped away from him upon impact and now lay five feet away.

With his side throbbing in pain, Cajun clawed, dragged, and pushed himself along the ground toward the gun. He heard his enemy approaching.

As Baehma charged into view, Cajun lunged for the gun, wrapping his hand over it and curling his finger around the trigger guard. He spun it around, slapped the handle into his palm, cocked the hammer, and fired.

Baehma's Smith & Wesson went off convulsively as Cajun's .45 slug caught him in the middle of his chest. The thick body teetered briefly, then fell back stiffly and hit the ground like a sack of stone.

Cajun forced himself to his knees, his Colt still trained. Then he let his gun arm sag. The man was dead.

RUSTLER'S BLOOD

David Everitt

LEISURE BOOKS ∞ NEW YORK CITY

A LEISURE BOOK

Published by

Dorchester Publishing Co., Inc.
6 East 39th Street
New York, NY 10016

Printed in the United States of America

1

Sloan was a town made up of one dirt road long enough to connect four buildings. One was a pinewood shack. On a warm fall night in 1879, harsh laughter could be heard coming from inside. Across the way was a provision storehouse made of stone and mortar. Next to that was the sheriff's office. Only two upright beams and one of the sides were standing now; the rest had been burned down three years earlier. The gutted frame sat eerily in the pale light coming from the shack—a last reminder of a time of order that seemed like ages ago. At the south end of the street was an adobe cantina. Inside four men were playing poker—two of the Claibournes, a kid named Tobey, and Cajun Lee.

Cajun Lee had just won his second hand in a row. Ike Claibourne looked ruefully at his losing hand as the stranger in the black serape took in the pot. Ike then turned to his brother.

"Why don't you sit out the next couple, Aaron?"

Aaron's broad forehead creased as he looked questioningly at his brother. He then darted a glance towards Cajun, nodded slowly in understanding, and got up from the table. Tobey turned to Cajun with a half smile, as if he were relishing some unspoken joke. The smile made him appear uglier than usual. He looked no more than eighteen, but his face could have belonged to an older man. It was long and pockmarked and set into a mean cast by slit eyes and a thin lined mouth.

Cajun shuffled the cards while noticing Aaron Claibourne amble up to the bar. Claibourne was trying to appear nonchalant about picking up the shotgun off the counter. He broke open the weapon and started cleaning the barrels.

Ike said, "Are we goin' to play cards, mister? Or are we goin' to moon over my brother all night?"

Tobey let out a spurt of laughter. "Hey, Aaron—I think you appeal to the stranger here."

Aaron looked up with his usual dull, thick look.

Cajun put out his cheroot and dealt the hands. The three men anted up, asked for their extra cards, and made their bets.

Then Ike Claibourne started going through the dead pile.

He picked up several cards and looked them over without any attempt to hide his actions. When he found one to his liking, he looked at Cajun squarely and put it into his hand. Following his example, Tobey reached out for the dead pile. Ike smacked the hand away.

"Now what's wrong with you, Tobey? You know you can't do that. That's cheating in the worst way." He turned to Cajun with a long grin. "Isn't it, mister?"

Cajun said nothing. The cheating so far had been nothing unusual. It had been discreet enough to be counted as fair play. Cajun had picked up some of the signs but let them slide because he could make up for them with a few tricks of his own. Now he just laid down his hand which had lost to Ike's full-house and pushed the deck to the middle of the table.

Ike said, "What's the matter, mister? You backing out just when my luck's beginning to change?"

"Like I said before, I'm just passing through on my way to Red Rock." Cajun doubted that this line would work but he thought it worth a try. "I've got a long ride tomorrow so I guess I'll find myself a place to bed down now."

Ike answered as Cajun started to get up, "You can't do that, mister. You've got to give me a chance to win some of my money back."

Aaron Claibourne dropped shells into the double barrels and closed the shotgun with a loud clink.

"I'll do the dealing for you," said Ike, "if that'll make it easier for you."

Cajun eased back into the chair. He watched Ike Claibourne start to shuffle, keeping his right hand under his serape. Ike began to chatter.

"So you're headed for Red Rock, are ya? It's a hell of a town, you can count on that. Leastways, it was when we came in." He grinned his half-smart smile again. "When you get there you should tell 'em you know us. Tell 'em you're friends of the Claibournes. They'd remember us—right, Aaron?"

Aaron nodded his head and laughed at some memory that gave him great pleasure. The cards were dealt out and then Aaron walked back to the table. He put one foot on his chair, laid the shotgun across his leg, and pointed it at Cajun, just in case the stranger hadn't gotten the message before.

Cajun rankled inside for having let himself get

7

into this position. This was a low form of robbery that he had heard of but had never actually come across before. They would take all his money and then have their fun with him, whether he provoked them or not. It took men who were especially mean and stupid to take pleasure in such an obvious routine and the three men sitting with Cajun now fit that description easily. That's what really bothered Cajun—that he had let his hunger for a few extra dollars get himself into a game with these rubes in the first place. A game with them was like getting into a pissing contest with a skunk.

For each play, Ike would find the extra card to his liking and complete some unbeatable hand. Once Cajun came up with a winning combination despite this, Ike then gave Tobey a shove, accused him of cheating and demanded the hand be played over.

Cajun placed the smallest bet possible on each play, drawing out this farce of a game as long as he could. Ike did not seem to mind. The longer the milking lasted, the more he enjoyed it.

"What's the matter, mister?" he would say with a chuckle. "You seem to be losing your touch."

Cajun had no illusion about being able to appease these men by just playing along. Neither did he think he would be any better off by just handing over his money outright. The only reason he went along with it was to stall until his best possible moment. There was no way these men would let him walk out, empty-handed or not.

He was soon down to his last ten dollars. He put in five for the new hand.

Ike said, "Come on, stranger. Don't be shy. Put it all in. We'll play double or nothing and then we

8

can be on our way."

Cajun put in the rest of his money. Tobey now decided to back out. He gave the man in the serape a fixed stare, a hand on his holster. When Ike found the cards to make a royal flush, the game was over. Out of the corner of his eye, Cajun could see Aaron Claibourne looking over the loot. Ike clapped his belly as if he had just finished a big meal.

"Well, mister, unless you got some more coins stashed in your boot, I think this here game is through."

As he looked into the stranger's piercing gray eyes, Ike's smile faded for the moment. He was suddenly overcome by an unexpected chill. A moment before he had been considering making the first move for his gun. Now he considered what might have been the outcome. He briefly imagined the bullet entering his body.

Ike caught himself on the thought and turned quickly to his brother.

"Take your share and then take this saddle tramp outside. He's a cheap bastard. We don't want to get his blood on the new floor."

Aaron nodded numbly in acknowledgement and then reached out to pick up some of the cash on the table. The time had come.

Aaron never saw the move. He heard the blast and the crack of the table as it was chipped by the shot from below. The .45 slug tore into his throat, then passed through his head and out the top of his skull.

Ike Claibourne jumped to his feet and grabbed his gun. Cajun swung the black Colt up and fired again. He had the bead on Ike but his target staggered suddenly to one side. Tobey had bolted for the back door and knocked Ike down on the way.

Ike fired as he hit the floor. The shot took an inch or two from Cajun's thigh. Cajun fanned the Colt twice, and Ike slammed back to the floor with the force of both shots.

Tobey was now shouldering his way through the rear door. The black Colt snapped off another shot but only splintered the door's wood frame. Cajun fired once more. He stood motionless for a moment as he stared through the empty doorway and listened to the bullet ricochet off a boulder and take off into the desert night air.

Tobey scrambled across the loose ground behind the cantina. At the other end of town he could see a shaft of light spring out from the shack as someone stepped outside. Tobey yelled to him and ran towards the light, glancing once behind to see if anybody was after him.

When he reached to shack he saw that it was Josh Claibourne standing outside. He was shirtless and bootless, and his pants were only half buttoned.

"Who's shootin'?" Josh said.

Tobey paused to catch his breath. "Ike and Aaron been murdered!"

Josh Claibourne grabbed him by the shirtfront and shook him. "What the hell you sayin'?"

"Stranger come in tonight. He come in on us in the cantina." He paused again. "He took our money and shot Ike and Aaron dead. I got out the back way."

Josh took off for the cantina at a run. Tobey could see him reach the back and freeze there as he looked inside. Then he came running back.

A rumble of hoofs came from the far end of the street. Tobey stepped quickly behind the shack and saw Cajun Lee sweep by at a gallop. The kid then hurried into the street to see the rider fade into the blackness. For the first time that night Tobey pulled out his gun. He fired once at the disappearing figure. The hoof-beats continued sounding into the desert.

Josh Claibourne came to the shack and turned inside. He grabbed his boots and shirt and gun belt and barked at the four men inside.

"Ike and Aaron been killed!"

The four men looked uncertainly at each other as Josh ran back out to get his horse. Then they pulled on their drawers and hurried to follow him outside. They left the Mexican girl sprawled on the floor. She made her way over to the corner where her clothes were heaped.

2

After Tobey ran out of the cantina, Cajun quickly pocketed the money on the table and went out the front. In the dark he had no trouble getting to his horse without being seen. He didn't know how many friends Ike and Aaron had in town so he played it safe and took his bay out at a gallop.

It was five miles outside of Sloan when Cajun first heard the riders somewhere behind. From the sound of it he figured they were five or six. He couldn't afford to make much of a study of the sound. They couldn't be more than a mile or two to his rear.

Up until then the land had been level enough for him to ride across without much trouble, but now the darkness and his lack of familiarity with this part of New Mexico was liable to take its toll. The moon was only half full that night but Cajun could still make out the rise up ahead. The top line was jagged and the rest of the incline was probably the same way. What he couldn't tell was how steep it was or if there were any trails leading through along the base.

When he drew his bay near he could see the least promising possibility had come true. The incline was steep and jagged, about four miles to the top. And there was no way around it, no paths along the base. There may have been some trails a few miles to either side, but in this blackness they would take too long to find. He smiled bitterly at his situation. He had stopped off at Sloan because he didn't want to try making it the rest of the way to Red Rock at night. Then he had gotten into the wrong game of poker—and here he was, after all!

He started the incline slowly, letting his mare feel its way along the rubble and gouges. He made a quarter mile in not much less than a half hour. He reined to a stop and dismounted to put his ear to the ground. The sounds were closer now. They would also slow up at the incline but they had to know the land pretty well. Cajun took the reins and led the horse on foot.

He almost took a dangerous spill on the edge of a rut while favoring the leg creased by Ike Claibourne's shot. He then made sure to pay more attention to the ground ahead, testing the ground himself, then leading the horse directly behind him. At the cry of a night bird the bay shied to one side. Cajun tried pulling her back on course and then felt the sudden tug on the reins. The animal keeled to one side, tried regaining its balance, then slipped to the ground with a heavy, sickening thud.

Cajun circled and saw the cause. A snake hole. He took a long sigh and crouched down slowly by the horse's side. As he came to the squatting position he felt as if his stomach kept sinking downward, falling lower and lower. He looked even though he knew he did not have to. The foreleg was broken. The horse was kicking. Cajun cursed as loud as he could dare to.

He would have to leave the animal now without doing what he should. The riders were probably

13

close enough to hear a shot and he was not carrying a knife. He pulled his Spencer repeater from its sheath, gathered up his canteen, and yanked the saddle bag out from underneath. He turned for a last look before walking on. The bay had served him well. She was worth a sight more than the two men he had killed in the cantina. He swung the saddle bag over his shoulder and started upward.

He came to the first flat piece, paused briefly to get his wind back and then moved on. He worked into a steady stride that he could keep up for some time. The rhythm of his progress was almost enough to clear his mind of the trouble he was headed for.

He had little doubt that, on horseback, he could have gotten away from the riders from Sloan and made it to some place where he could have lain low until the pursuers decided to give up the search. He then could have made the last stretch to Red Rock and, if luck was still with him, the silver mine boom would still be on. The business in Sloan would have been just another regrettable run-in and he would have had his chance at the boom town's easy money. But now that he was afoot it would only be a matter of time till he was overtaken. Cajun didn't think much about why he kept on moving. What he would do when he was found he wasn't even willing to guess at.

He kept his pace up for another hour. He stopped to judge how much further it was to the top of the ridge. It had to be at least another two miles. Then he heard a shot from down below. The riders had found his horse.

As the bay mare gave out its final spasmodic

kick, Josh Claibourne put the smoking pistol back in his belt. He turned along with his brother Amos and Nick Laughlin and Morgan Fleet to watch the two stragglers catch up.

Nick said, "She couldn't have gone down more than an hour ago, maybe an hour and a half."

Josh turned his gaze towards the dark incline. "Well, he sure as hell ain't going far just walkin'. It won't be much longer now."

Tobey and Jesse Laughlin made the last ridge and reined their animals alongside the dead mare. Jesse swung slowly out of the saddle.

He said, "We ain't after much of a horseman if he lets his animal's leg get broke like that."

"The way you ride him," said Josh, "your horse ain't going to last long either. Better stay off him for awhile. Your fat butt'll kill him yet."

"I don't know that I'll last much longer either. Tobey, you got some hard-tack? I need something to fill me."

Tobey said he didn't. The same went for the rest of them. They hadn't taken the time to bring anything with them other than their guns. Jesse complained some more about tiredness.

|Nick said, "What's the matter, Jess? That little greaser bitch wore you out?" His laughter was joined by Morgan.

"She was something though, wasn't she?" said Jesse. "And I'll be damned if she didn't start to like it herself after awhile, long around the second time through."

"You better watch it," said Morgan. "You better not take to her too much. I think Johnny Baehma was starting to take a shine to her before he went south. He might have words with you if he

15

finds out what you're thinking.''

"Over a Mex? What're you saying? Johnny Baehma don't fight over them. That's what he. . .''

"Shut your foul mouth,'' snapped Amos. Jesse stopped his talking and no one else bothered speaking either. "I'm tired of your worldly thoughts, especially at a time like this!''

Amos Claibourne was the only one in the family who took his biblical name seriously. It was never clear why Old Man Claibourne had given all his sons names from the Old Testament, but Amos was sure it meant they had received some sort of call. He would tell the others about it often and at great length. He was rarely interrupted, partly because his kin really didn't understand all that he was saying and partly because no one had dared get into a fight with him for six years. He had that lean, unpredictable strength of a man whose mind had turned at an early age. He went on:

"And coming from you too, Jesse. Ike and Aaron were cousins of yours. You heard what Tobey said. This stranger from the desert came to our home and killed two of our own out of greed of their money—''

Josh Claibourne took a few steps up the slope to take a look at the trail. He figured they could walk the horses another half mile and then mount up and cut down the distance for sure. When they came close they could leave the horses and go on foot and smoke out the bastard wherever they found him. The Old Man had taught them to take care of their own and they all knew what was expected of them. Josh scratched his beard while considering what they could do with the stranger when they caught up. Like all the Claibournes and their relations, the Laughlins, his thoughts ran wild when considering what could be done to people outside the family. After a few moments of this he returned to the bunch. Amos was still holding them with his talk.

"—And this is the most unpardonable sin of all, murder. Murder of one of us! We must have that eye for the eye. And you talk about the concubine back in town!"

He stopped himself. His eyes wavered slightly from side to side, then he grasped the three inch thick gold cross around his neck. Private thoughts had a grip on him, thoughts of the turn he had taken with the Mexican girl.

Like the others he took hold of the reins on his horse and the six men from Sloan led their animals upward in silence.

When he neared the top of the ridge, Cajun stopped short to pick up the sound. He didn't have to put an ear to the ground to hear the approaching horses anymore.

He surveyed the land around him. Here the surface was at its most irregular and craggy. It was as good a place to pick as any. He skirted along the ridge about ten feet below its top to find his best cover. If he topped the slope now he could leave himself revealed against the background of the sky. Just behind a scalloped rise, he slid the saddle bag off his shoulder and knelt down.

He peered through the darkness, trying to pick out any moving | shadow further down. The rasp of hoof-falls continued. The fact that Cajun could not see anyone did not mean that they were not close at hand. The broken landscape could easily conceal them until they were right on top of him. Judging from the strength of the sound, they could be anywhere between a half mile and accurate firing range.

Cajun loaded up the Spencer and checked the cylinder of his Colt. He kept his downhill watch for fifteen minutes. Then he saw a head bob up from behind a boulder.

It was the head of a man moving on foot, about a hundred feet off. A few seconds later Cajun saw two other shadows of men afoot, climbing in a slow crouch. Their horses must have been left behind. That meant that they knew Cajun was nearby.

Now with the men from Sloan closing in, Cajun felt more in control of the situation. He wasn't dealing with something formless anymore. Here was something he could scheme against. His mind began sizing up the options.

He couldn't stay where he was and hope they would pass by, and he couldn't hope to fight them off from this vantage point. He considered the downward slope of the formation before him. It narrowed as it went downhill. At its lowpoint it looked to be about two feet high. Past that it built up again and leveled off at around five feet. In all, the winding formation stretched for about twenty feet. After snaking past the lowpoint, Cajun might be able to move downhill enough to slip past the men as they climbed up. If he could do that, he should be able to find the horses, take one for himself, scare the rest off, and go down the way he came.

He saw another form circling to his left some thirty feet away. He got down on his belly and put

18

his plan into motion, crawling off to his right.

When he came to the dip in the formation Cajun stopped. At the bottom end of the path another shadow appeared. It took a step in Cajun's direction, then hesitated. Cajun flattened himself against the stoney floor. The shadow stood still for many long moments. After another tentative step, it turned and stole around to the other side of the formation and out of Cajun's sight. Cajun waited several seconds, then continued down.

As the crest rose, he lifted himself to a crouch and walked bent-kneed. This wasn't any faster than a crawl, but with the length of his body dragging along the ground he was liable to make more noise.

He came to another stop when footsteps neared from above. They stopped alongside the top of the crest and were soon joined by another pair. There was a faint whisper. One pair of footsteps then moved straight away from the crest and the other moved uphill.

Cajun went for the last seven feet. He made it without any more contact. At the end of the formation, he side-stepped to his left and took a look at the other side. The nearest movement was fifteen feet uphill. The lead man was topping the ridge and becoming outlined against the sky. Cajun counted five altogether, but couldn't be sure.

He went into a crouch and darted for the rock five feet down. Following a line of cover, he made the point where he figured he'd first sighted one of the party. He stayed put until he got his next lead. To the left and down he heard a horse's snort. He moved to the next cover and from there could see the horses grouped by a cottonwood. He took a step onward.

Then he heard the man to his side.

Cajun wheeled. A short piece away he could make out the indistinct outline against a dim landscape. Across the man's body was the thinner line of a rifle. Time was suspended as both men stood frozen, trying to make out the target before them. Then Cajun dropped to his knees, deliberately creating a sudden sound. The other man went for it. He fired and the shot whizzed above Cajun's head. The flare from the barrel gave Cajun his bull's eye. He levered and fired the Spencer twice. The shadow across from him spun and dropped. Cajun was running before the man hit the ground.

Shouts came from his rear. A moment later he could hear the hard, fast footfalls of men running. The horses were a few yards off, becoming jittery. Suddenly Cajun was aware of footsteps bearing down directly behind him.

He turned, but could only see the sharp rise between him and the sound. The man from Sloan had to be coming across the flat piece leading to the top of the rise. Cajun rushed to the base of the drop and flattened himself against its side. He heard another last footfall on the ground above him. The man took a running jump off the top of the rise. Cajun fired up along the arc of the jump. The man twisted in mid-air. He came down hurting.

With the shot, the horses bolted. Cajun took after them. A horse crossed his path with the reins dragging on the ground. Cajun lunged for the reins. He ended up sprawling with a mouthful of dirt. He came up empty-handed and the horse made off across the incline.

Guns sounded and bullets kicked up dirt at his

feet. Cajun zigzagged to one side as the men closed in. He felt a sudden yank on his shoulder and he stumbled to his left. He was hit. Up ahead was a boulder. He dove and tumbled behind its cover.

Rifle fire ricocheted off the rock as Cajun checked his left shoulder. The bullet had gone clean through. He braced himself to return the barrage. The gunshots paused. Cajun levered the Spencer and straightened to the top of the boulder, lining himself against the direction of the fire. He stopped before getting off the first shot.

The men were no longer there.

He turned to the sounds coming from downhill. Someone was dragging the wounded man by the base of the rise. The others were going after the horses. Cajun watched them running down and getting smaller in the distance. He then slumped against the rock.

He wanted to stay exactly where he was and never move. But he knew he did not have that choice. When his system slowed down a bit, he set off in the best direction he knew—away from Sloan. At the time he was sure he would never come this way again.

3

Only three of the horses were found which made the return to Sloan a slow and bitter affair. With a slug lodged in his hip, Josh Claibourne rated a ride for the distance, leaving only two animals for Amos, Tobey, Jesse Laughlin, and Morgan Fleet. Nick's corpse was draped over the saddle for the first two miles; then, reasoning he had no cause to object at this point, the others roped the body to the saddle horn and dragged it alongside, to give one of the survivors some relief from walking. Another few miles further on, Jesse said they couldn't let his brother's body be mutilated anymore by the drag of the ground underneath and Amos went on to point out the Claibournes weren't the kind to let that sort of thing happen to one of their kin. They left the dead man in a gully, promising to fetch him back to town later so they could bury him proper.

They haggled and swore their way back to Sloan and didn't reach the outskirts until the sun was high in the sky the next day. Within sight of the cantina the group stopped as one. Outside the drinking place were hitched five horses, still lathered and spent, one of them a gray, thick-muscled steeldust. Even Josh realized through his fazing pain that explanations had to be made.

The party tramped over to the cantina, eased Josh out of the saddle and walked through the door. Inside they found Johnny Baehma with the rest at the bar.

Baehma was flanked on one side by Sol Claibourne and Levi Ruffner and on the other by Billy and Ave Laughlin. The acrid smell of gunpowder and blood was still in the room from the night before. Johnny Baehma studied the returning group slowly and downed a half-glass of mescal. With the sting of the drink, his wide face bunched into sudden lines, then relaxed into its usual hard planes. The long green eyes flicked across the faces of the men by the door.

He said, "We put Ike and Aaron out back. What happened?"

Tobey started it off with the story about the stranger in the black serape coming into town the night before and gunning down the two Claibournes, then Jesse took it up, telling about the ride into the mountains and the fight there. After it was all told there was silence. Jesse, Tobey, Amos and Morgan Fleet avoided Baehma's stare, finding something to occupy them by laying Josh out on a row of three chairs. Morgan mumbled something about making a poultice for the wound.

"You ran after the horses," Baehma snapped. "And while you were running that son of a bitch got away."

"The Huecas Mountains is a long way," Jesse said weakly. "We couldn't walk the whole way."

Baehma's eyes locked coldly on the fat man. Amos spoke fast.

"The signs were not right. Cousin Nick was taken from us to show us the luck of the Lord was

23

not with us. Our time was still waiting and if we was to—"

Johnny Baehma threw his glass hard to the side, smashing it against the adobe wall. For the next few moments the cantina was all quiet again.

"I won't have none of that now, Amos! Two Claibournes and a Laughlin are killed and the one that did it is still walkin'. The Old Man taught you better than that. He taught you all better."

Baehma waited for a reply. Tobey lowered his eyes and scratched idly at a spot beneath his ribs, Jesse sat heavily on a bench, and Morgan Fleet glanced at Amos to make sure that he was holding his tongue. Johnny went on.

"People are always trying to push us out, you all know that. We have something special and we got to hold on just that much more to keep it that way. Someone's got to see to that. The Old Man would disown you in a minute if he could see you now."

Baehma stopped again to let this have its effect.

When Johnny Baehma rode into Chavero County four years ago, he was known as a dangerous man with a gun who had put his talents to use in the cattle towns and range wars in Texas. His reasons for leaving Texas were not clear. There was a rumor that it was a secret because Johnny had good reason to keep it that way. This did not bother Old Man Claibourne. He welcomed the renegade into his outfit with enthusiasm, within a few months making Baehma his chief lieutenant. Johnny assumed leadership of the outlaw clan two years later after the Old Man was killed in ambush on one of his rustling forays to the south. Since then Baehma had learned that he could keep his thumb on all the profitable outlaw activities in the area just as long as he could keep the Old Man's creed alive.

Amos, Jesse, Morgan, and Tobey had come into the cantina feeling as if they couldn't take another step. The four men with Johnny didn't feel much stronger. But now they were all finishing their drinks and checking their loads. Baehma watched with a twist of a smile as they dragged themselves towards the door. These men would do anything for you if you handled them right.

Baehma had another mescal while the others found fresh mounts and sent for the doctor to tend to Josh, now passed out where he had been left. The outlaw chief then picked up a heavy sack from the other side of the bar, crossed to the other end of the street to store it away in the pinewood shack, and joined the others saddling up outside the old sheriff's office.

Once on top of his animal, Morgan Fleet turned to Johnny with a glint of hope in his eye. "Have a lucky time across the border, Johnny?"

Baehma swung on to the gray steeldust and scanned the eight faces turned in his direction. "You can say that. Yes sir, we are going to have us some time up in Red Rock this month—are we ever!" He turned his horse towards the north, towards the Huecas, and started off at a trot, the others close behind.

Tobey brought his horse up to the lead. "Anyone try to keep the stuff from you, Johnny?"

"There were around six of them that tried."

Ave Laughlin whistled under his breath. "God damn, but them greasers sure like to bleed though, don't they?"

Robles let out a quiet, tired breath before answering. "You won't be seeing me there," he said. "I will leave it to other men."

Jorge Lucero settled back in his chair and leveled an insistent stare on his neighbor. He had expected this response but he had promised the others he would try once more. "Why don't you at least come to the meeting and listen to us. That is not asking much, is it?"

"I have nothing to listen to. There is nothing they can tell me that I don't know. I know as much as anyone else about what the Sloan gang has been up to. But my way is different, that's all."

Lucero accepted the cup of coffee from Robles' wife and gazed at the surface of the drink until words would come to him. It wasn't going to be easy to come up with a new argument. There wasn't much you could do to get a man to give up his own very personal sort of pride.

Robles waited tolerantly as his visitor sorted things out in his mind. Robles didn't have much use for the man, but as long as Lucero was at his table he would let him say his piece.

Diego Robles' ranch was southwest of Sloan, about ten miles away, just on the other side of the Rio Gallino. He had come there with his wife, three children, and younger sister six years earlier, before the silver strike up north and the sudden influx of fortune seekers in the region. Like the other older settlers in Chavero County, Robles was leery of the newcomers, even those who proved themselves honest. His business in cattle made enough for him to live on with a little to spare and he figured his ranch would stay on and amount to something

26

more—which, to his mind, put him several notches above all those drifters, whatever they happened upon.

There were other Mexicans established in the area and many times the worst offenses of the Sloan bunch were directed at them. Robles was as outraged at these crimes as anyone but he couldn't see having any part of Lucero's vigilante group. Robles had lived north of the border his whole life, spoke English as well as he did Spanish, and knew as much about the ways of the United States as any Anglo did. He considered himself an American, even toyed with the idea of running for office one day. He wouldn't ride around with a pack of wild-eyed men bent on shooting anything gringo.

"Perhaps," Lucero said, "you do not understand how important a man like yourself would be to us. Diego, a man of your ability, he could do much for us."

Robles didn't like to be flattered in this way. He turned towards the near window and ignored the man across from him by training his eyes on some movement on the horizon. Lucero continued.

"You could lead us, Diego. We need that. I do not know how to lead this group of men. And if we don't do something soon, it may be too late, for all of us. What we need now is—"

Lucero's talk grew, but, for Robles, it quickly dimmed into the background. At first the recognition was vague, but as the figure on the horizon approached he was gripped by the feeling of something gone terribly wrong. When the figure staggered towards the outer corral, he came to his feet suddenly.

"Luisa," he said.

He rushed out the door, swung up on his pinto, and galloped over to the outer corral. He found his sister bruised and shaken, with shredded clothes and a story about going to stay with a neighbor last night and instead spending the evening in a pinewood shack in Sloan.

Robles left her with his wife, then rode out with Lucero to attend a meeting nearby.

4

On its northeast side, the Huecas sloped down in sharp broken steps, rose once again into a long scalloped rise, then dipped into a great expanse. Clawing to the top of the rise, Cajun could see the ranch on the flats below.

It was a place with money behind it. The central white shingle house had two stories with a covered porch running along all four sides. The materials for the building looked to have been brought out from the east. To one side were two bunkhouses, the stable and the corrals. To the other, situated closer to the house, was a cleared rectangle designed for lounging that was surrounded by the best garden one could expect from the region. Stretching beyond all this was good grazing land. Cajun's eyes rested on one of the corrals holding ten or twelve horses. With his stake from last night's poker game he would be able to buy one, along with some supplies. With effort he lifted himself to his feet and started down.

The bleeding from his shoulder had slowed but he had already lost enough blood to make him weak. After nearly tumbling, he paused and continued on at a deliberate pace, turning into a gradually sloping draw and steadying himself with a hand on his side. He came to a bend in the route, turned for the last leg to the flats, then heard a metallic click to his back and left. He stopped short, heard another click to his right, another to his rear.

Cajun knew it couldn't be the men from Sloan. He would have picked up the signs if they had still been trailing him. Holding the Spencer by its barrel, he slowly raised his arm, bringing the weapon a couple of feet from his body; and then, just as slowly, he turned around.

A man on top of a roan came down into the draw, keeping his carbine leveled at Cajun. Two other horsemen, also with carbines, rode into view from either side. They studied Cajun in silence. Cajun let them speak first.

The man on the roan simply said, "You're on 'the Tolfane place."

Little else was needed to be said. Cajun had no doubts about what the Tolfanes thought of uninvited guests.

"I want to buy a horse," said Cajun. "It looked like you could spare one."

The rider on the right moved in for a closer look at the stranger. The horseman was a round-shouldered, compactly built man. His smooth, clean shaven face was made distinctive by the close, deep-set eyes and the seemingly natural curl to his lip. He said, "How come you don't have one, mister?"

"That makes no difference. The money's the same."

"Looks like a lot of bleeding from your shoulder. Where'd you find the trouble?"

"That's no difference either."

The rider came at Cajun a couple more steps,

answering."

Cajun could see no advantage in acting as if he needed to explain. "I've told you all you need to know."

The rider's face darkened. He started for Cajun again.

"Hold it, Phin."

It was the man on the roan. Phin jerked his head towards him, then back at Cajun, his fingers flexing around his reins in agitation.

"This fella needs to learn how to talk, Lafe."

"I haven't seen him with Baehma before," said Lafe. "And Baehma doesn't bring in anyone from outside." He lowered his carbine and slid it into his saddle boot. "We'll take him down. He can talk to Mr. Tolfane."

Lafe and the man on the left led the way through the draw. Phin swung his horse around and blocked Cajun's path for a moment. He spat on Cajun's shadow, then moved aside to let him through, riding a few feet to his rear.

Cajun was brought to the far side of the house, led in through the back door, and taken into the kitchen where he was left to wait while Lafe went further inside to find his boss. A few minutes later a silver-haired man wearing a gray suit stepped into the kitchen.

"My name is Burt Tolfane. Is there something I can do for you?"

He was a slim man who carried himself with a sense of importance that seemed to fit. As the stranger told him what he needed, Tolfane's black eyes took in the red hole in the serape and the swath across the leg. For a moment he looked at Cajun without seeming to hear him, then cut him

31

then reined himself short. "We ain't asking questions to pass the time, mister. You better try off, ordering his men to take Cajun into a guest room and to bring in the head servant.

Cajun was left in the room with the servant who began to dress the two wounds. It was clearly work that the man had done before. Judging from what he had seen of the region, Cajun guessed that he had done it recently. He wasn't, however, able to guess why it was being done for him, though for the time being he was perfectly willing to accept it. Tolfane returned when the job was nearly done. The silver-haired man brought with him a tray of food which he placed alongside the patient.

Sitting in an overstuffed chair, Tolfane said, "I hope you'll overlook the way my men acted towards you when they saw you coming."

Cajun said he hadn't given it much thought.

"I'm glad to hear it. They have a job to do and at times some of them become a little overzealous, I'm afraid. There's no excuse for the way Phin acted to you when you so obviously were in need of help. As to your requests, when you are patched up and revived, you can feel free to look over my stock and pick out the animal that appeals to you. I can also provide you with food and any other supplies you may need to get you where you want to go. I'm sure we can arrive at a reasonable price."

The servant secured the last bandage, gathered up his equipment, and left the room. Tolfane watched with narrowed eyes as Cajun got to work on the steak and eggs before him.

"May I ask where you'll be going when you leave here?"

"I'm on my way to Red Rock."

32

"I see, right into the thick of it. It seems that's where all the young men are going. I suppose I would too if I were your age. That's where all the activity is."

"So I've heard."

"There's so much there that it seems to spill over into the surrounding areas. Why, just last night we got a piece of it in Sloan."

"Is that right?"

"Oh yes. One of my men was through there this afternoon and got the story from the fellow who works at the provision store. It seems two of the Claibournes were killed."

Cajun brought the cup of coffee to his mouth, returning Tolfance's steady gaze.

"The way my man heard it, there was a fight over cards, between the Claibournes and some stranger. The stranger was supposed to be a big bear of a man, somewhere around six foot five and nearly as wide. He took at least four bullets but kept on blazing away with his two Colts and cut both men down. He must have been bleeding rivers but he rode out of town with the rest of the gang on his tail."

"Sounds like quite a story."

"Well, to tell you the truth, I think it's been blown up. I know the two Claibournes were killed, but I doubt it was done quite that way. No, the way I figure, this stranger was no giant. A tall man maybe, about six feet, but hard and thin. He's no bear. And that thing about four bullets—my guess is it was more like two, like one through the shoulder and the other across the thigh."

Cajun put down the knife and fork and leaned back on the couch.

33

"Later on," Tolfane said, "I heard that the stranger got away, going north. He would probably travel through the Huecas. He might angle northeast and end up here." He waited a moment for a response. "Am I right?"

"You're right."

"I also see that it was only one Colt that was put to work."

"You're right there also. Now let me ask you something. You know there's a gang after me. Why'd you take me in?"

Tolfane got up and, crossing over to a cabinet, took out a bottle of brandy and poured himself a glass. Once while in New Orleans, Cajun had developed a taste for brandy and he expected to be offered a glass here. He wasn't.

Tolfane said, "I must confess to you, I have a personal interest in this. And in you in particular, Mr.—perhaps now that you see that I already know a certain amount about you, you won't mind me asking your name."

"It's Lee. You can call me Cajun Lee."

"Cajun, eh? That means you're French, am I right?"

"Something like that."

"From Louisiana, isn't it? A very interesting people. We must talk about it sometime."

"Sometime."

"Of course. I don't blame you for wanting to get to the point." He returned to his chair, leaning on its back. "For years this part of the country has been the home for a tenacious, tightly knit outlaw bunch. They were always a bad group to deal with, but since the silver strike they have become ten times worse. With all the easy money and the

34

desperate new recruits, these men have been on a rampage for four solid years. Since the sheriff was murdered by Johnny Baehma three years ago there has been absolutely nothing in their way. Our only respite has been those times when they head up to Red Rock to have their idea of a good time." He took a delicate sip from his glass, paused to savor the taste. "As you can see, Mr. Lee, something has to be done. And the only recourse is for private citizens to make a stand. That is why I am interested in you. Those three men you came across in the hills are not ordinary ranch hands. They are specially selected range detectives whom I've hired in the past few months to protect my property and to maintain as much order as possible in the rest of the area. As of now, I have seven men—the three you saw and four others who are out guarding my stock. I could use another. You've given the Claibournes and Laughlins a nasty bite. They'd think twice if I had someone like you on my side."

Cajun finished his last sip of coffee. "I appreciate all you've done, Mr. Tolfane, but I'm going to turn down your offer."

"Mr. Lee, if it's the idea of being a hired gun that offends you, you can rest easy. What I want is a group of men who can keep things in line with as little violence as possible. With the reputation you now have around here, you'd be just the man."

"That's not the problem, Mr. Tolfane."

"What is it, the money? I assure you, I pay well."

"I don't doubt it. But I don't work for wages." He came to his feet. "I'll be on my way to Red Rock. The money may not be as certain, but I'd rather take my chances."

Cajun started for the door as Tolfane replied. "I think I could make it worth your while. Perhaps it's only the terms we have to go over."

The door opened as Cajun was about to say his mind was set. Lafe took two quick steps into the room.

"What is it, Jenkins?" asked Tolfane.

"It's Baehma and the rest. They're riding in."

"It seems, Mr. Lee, that they haven't given up."

"I could take a horse in the back," said Cajun. "I could still lose them."

Putting an arm out, Lafe stopped Cajun by the door. "Forget it. They're too close." He turned to Tolfane. "With just three of us here, we'll have to let them come in. We'll cover 'em from the windows."

"Go to it. Take Mr. Lee with you. Stay with him."

Lafe sent the two other range detectives to opposite corner windows. Going up the stairs with Lafe to a room overlooking the corral, Cajun wondered whether the range detective was supposed to protect him or just keep an eye on him. At the window facing the hills, he could see there was a more pressing problem to be handled first.

Nine riders were coming to a dusty stop by the near corral. Cajun recognized the kid Tobey somewhere to the rear. After some orders from the man at the front, the group walked their horses around to the front of the house, breaking up into two parties. Lafe handed Cajun his Spencer.

"You can make yourself useful, if it comes to it." The detective then placed himself alongside another front window on the other side of the room. Outside, one of the riders called out for

Tolfane. The rancher stepped out of the front door, unarmed, and came down off the porch, looking a bit irritated but otherwise pretty unconcerned about all the guns before him.

"What do you want, Baehma?"

"We're looking for someone. We thought he might've come by here."

"A stranger came by this afternoon, but that's no concern of yours."

"It is if he was wearing a black serape."

"That sounds like him, but that doesn't change anything."

"Is that right, Tolfane? Well, maybe me and the fellas should take a look around."

"I don't think you want to, Baehma."

The two range detectives on the ground floor poked their carbines through the windows, trained on Johnny Baehma. Lafe and Cajun followed suit upstairs. Baehma's face reddened. He swore and threatened Tolfane. The rancher calmly asked Baehma if there was anything else he could for him. The rest of the men from Sloan watched the windows uneasily while Baehma glared at the silver-haired man. Swinging his steeldust around, the outlaw chief then rode away from the house a short piece with the other men grouping around him to talk things over. Tolfane stepped back on to the porch.

Half-turning to Cajun, Lafe said, "A cool customer that Tolfane, ain't he?"

Cajun said that he was. He asked who the leader of the Sloan bunch was.

"That be Johnny Baehma. Ever hear of him?"

"Once or twice before today."

Cajun studied the broad-faced, broad-shouldered man settling down his henchmen. He made a mental note of the way the two guns were positioned on his hips and noted the deep-pocketed jacket that probably held something more. He also took a moment to admire the fast animal underneath the outlaw.

Cajun said, "Is he as good as they say?"

"I don't know what to tell you. Most people are scared to hell of him. He's supposed to be some kind of lightning with those Smith & Wessons of his—but to tell you the truth, from what I've heard, he doesn't shoot unless he's got the drop."

"That makes him dangerous enough."

"That's for sure. There's plenty of greasers will tell you that. Baehma and a few of the others just came back north from dropping a few more. It was a hijacking. Some Mex had traded for a shipment of silver up north and was bringing it back home when Baehma found him. Six were killed and I hear those Sloan boys like to do it slow."

Cajun turned slowly toward Lafe. He left his question unasked when he saw the Sloan gang coming back towards the porch.

Baehma said, "We're goin' to let you have this one, Tolfane. But we'll be comin' back, you can put money on it. You won't know when it'll be—but when we do, whether that son of a bitch is here or not, we'll take this place apart."

Tolfane said that he was welcome to try and the two of them traded remarks back and forth once more before the Sloan party turned round and headed back for home.

When they saw them ride into the hills, Lafe and Cajun left their posts and started down the stairs. Cajun asked if the stolen silver shipment was big enough to warrant a posse of some kind from the south. The range detective said that 20,000 dollars worth was big enough, but the Mexicans were probably too leery of the Sloan bunch to try anything.

Cajun weighed 20,000 against his prospects up in Red Rock.

Tolfane poured himself another brandy when he walked into his study. He usually didn't have too much trouble bracing himself to stand up to Baehma, but he was always left with the jitters as soon as it was over. He was considering a second glass when Lafe and Cajun Lee came through the doorway.

For a moment, the rancher was struck by something different in the stranger. After a quick looking-over, he located the change. It was the twist of a smile almost hidden by the black moustache.

"Well, Mr. Lee, I think you can feel free to go. I do hope, though, that you reconsider my proposition just once more."

Stepping towards the rancher, Cajun said, "Actually, Mr. Tolfane, I have reconsidered. Watching you out there speaking up for me against Johnny Baehma and the rest, I got to thinking." Cajun picked up the bottle next to Tolfane and found a glass on the near shelf. "I said to myself, this man is really putting himself on the line for me."

"I was only doing what had to be done."

"Maybe." Cajun filled his glass. "But it was more than you'll get from most people. I have an obligation to you, Mr. Tolfane, and I think the best thing I can do to repay you is to help in any way I can with the trouble you're having here."

"Well, you know that you're welcome to join us."

"I appreciate that," Cajun said. He sipped the brandy, then downed the rest in one gulp, relishing the smooth path it forged down into his stomach. He thought that this part of the country might not be so bad after all.

5

Gallino Station was a little more than twenty miles south of Sloan, on the northern side of the toll bridge. Joe Anson owned the station and collected the tolls and paid tribute to Johnny Baehma for both. Once Anson tried getting out of a payment and lost two fingers on his left hand. Baehma later told him he regretted what Amos Claibourne had done and, by way of making it up to him, let him have one of Amos' recently rustled horses. Anson could have sold out and left the territory, but the sorrel pleased him and, even with the tribute, the Claibourne-Laughlin crowd brought him a fair business. Next to Sloan, Gallino Station was their favorite haunt. They'd eat, and gambling there for days at a time whenever they had reason to pass through the Ruffner and Laughlin ranches nearby.

The day after riding to Tolfane's ranch, part of the clan had come in and Amos, Jesse, Sol, and Morgan Fleet were still playing monte by ten o'clock that night. Even if they had been paying attention, they probably wouldn't have noticed the armed men stealing about in the darkness outside.

Along the side of the stable, three men with rifles moved forward towards the corner opposite the back of the station. Four more crawled behind the cover of the bank of the river, splitting into twos, one pair following the bend in the Gallino towards the west side of the station, the other angling towards the front door. Some twenty-five feet from the door, Robles put a hand on his companion's arm to bring him to a stop.

The impact of the news of the rape in Sloan on the meeting the day before had been decisive. Most of the Mexicans were on the verge of a final violent commitment to the vigilante cause, and Robles' story had been more than enough to tip the scales. As offensive as all the other depredations had been, never before had the Sloan gang gone as far as violating a respectable Mexican woman. The plans for revenge were immediate. Having served in a campaign against the Comanche, Robles was the logical choice for jefe.

Over the top of the river bank Robles could make out the card game in progress through the window. He waited the time alloted for Lucero and the other two to take their positions at the stable.

He checked the chambers in his Colt and for no particularly good reason checked the action of his Henry. It had been years since he was last in combat and he wasn't as confident as he thought he should be. The other men were unknown quantities, but they at least knew how to shoot—if not at men. Still, considering the sound plan and the odds, that experience should prove to be enough.

From Luisa, Robles learned the identities of the men who had taken her. Speaking to a trader who had just passed through Sloan, he then found out about Amos, Sol, Jesse, and Morgan going south for fresh horses at the Laughlin place. Here was enough information for him to put his plans into motion. Now there were four men inside, seven of his own on the outside, another holding the horses in the hills and five others below Sloan to hold off any more of the gang thinking of riding down. A foolproof set-up. What Robles didn't know was that Johnny Baehma was sleeping it off in the station's back room.

Robles checked his watch. The time Lucero needed to set himself up had passed. Robles and the man next to him, Urbina, climbed over the bank. As they silently advanced towards the station, the two men opposite the west wall started forward as well.

Four horses were hitched by the front door. Robles and Urbina drew within ten feet without stirring them, dropping behind a trough that was in a direct line with the window showing the card game inside. The two from the further bank came to the side wall to Robles' left.

Lucero would wait for the first shot. He was the insurance in case anyone tried going out the back door to get to the horses in either the rear corral or the stable. With a better chance than those at the side, Robles and Urbina brought up their rifles. As he trained his sights on Sol Claibourne, Robles thought he picked up the faint sound of feet scuffling across sand. A shot from a Winchester then roared from somewhere to the front of the stable. Glass shattered. Robles swore and fired desperately while the four men inside flattened against the floor.

His instincts at work while fitfully asleep, Johnny Baehma swept a hand under the pillow and rolled off the mattress at the first crack of gunfire. He hit the floor with a Smith & Wesson balanced in the palm of his hand.

He lay motionless at first, trying to place the direction of the shots. Straight ahead. The side of the station. From the stable. Someplace further off. Also to the front.

Walking in a crouch, he reached the side window and peered out. A Mexican was behind a boulder about thirty feet from the station, firing at a front window. He looked familiar. Baehma remembered some of the boys having a little fun with him once when he didn't have the money to pay the toll for crossing the bridge. Lopez was his name. By the stable were two others, one firing, the other yelling at Lopez to get back.

The outlaw chief left the window, walking low towards the door, where the rest of the noise was coming from. The main room was in a shambles. The table in the corner was overturned, shards of glass were strewn along the floor, bottles were shattered, the oil lamp was shot down. While Anson huddled behind the bar, Baehma's men emptied their chambers out the windows. Sol Claibourne, ducking under a renewed barrage from the front, turned to Baehma.

"Shit, Johnny, what're we gonna do?"

Two shots whizzed threw the front window, sending pots and platters skidding off the bar. More of them pelted the side wall. Baehma dashed to Morgan's side, turning behind the overturned table for cover when something caught his eye. Across the room, on the quiet side, through the front window he caught a glimpse of a passing broad-brimmed hat and the loose sleeve of a shirt. Two gun muzzles crashed through the glass and Baehma moved.

44

In a single continuous motion, he dove for the opposite wall, spun over on his shoulder and came up behind a chair in line with the window, his Smith & Wesson bellowing. He triggered four times. The muzzles disappeared. In a brief pause in the gunfire there could be heard an anguished moan.

Baehma charged the window, saw the two Mexicans scrambling off, one keeping the other on his feet. The outlaw tried another shot, but the healthy Mexican kept him low with pistol fire, dragging his friend to the protection of a deep cut.

Baehma figured these two had been cut off from the action by the windowless west wall and had only just now gotten up the nerve to make a play. That meant there were besiegers on all sides. Creeping back to the table, he sent his last two rounds toward the trough and reloaded, looking out each side, searching for an opening.

Lopez levered two more shots and bolted for the rear corner of the station. The two by the stable gave up on ordering him back, firing wildly as they ran out, diving toward the safety at the back of the building where they would join their comrade.

Thumbing in the last cartridge, Baehma now saw his chance.

"We're getting out," he barked.

He ran to the back room and picked up his second pistol.

"What the hell are you doing?"

"A man can wait just so long," Lopez said over his shoulder. "I deserved the first shot."

The fire from the front kept up. Lucero won-

45

dered how long those two could last behind the meager cover of the trough. He also wondered how he could explain this to Robles when it was over.

"Lopez," he said, "watch the door. Antonio and I, we'll go up and try to get close to the side window."

Lucero fed in more cartridges and tried to figure what the two on the other side would do. He levered in the next load and pulled Antonio towards the front—but then the back door flew open.

He wheeled to see Johnny Baehma spring out, a gun in each hand.

The left one spoke. Lopez twisted, slammed against the wall, his rifle discharing at the sky.

Lucero and Antonio swung their guns around. Three shots rattled from the Smith & Wessons. Antonio hurtled back and dropped sprawling to the ground. Lucero thudded down, his belly torn through.

Lucero struggled to arch his head up. Scrambling feet swept past him. He could hear the creak of the corral gate opening. Dust filled his eyes and his body shook with pain.

Pressing the stock of the Henry to his shoulder, Robles aimed for the corner of the window where he had last seen a hand gun raised. He waited, then lowered the weapon, taking hold of Urbina's arm.

"No firing. They're not firing."

Urbina listened with him. Their man to the left fired once, then stopped too. In the sudden silence, Robles heard a horse whinny and hoofs hit the ground, not in confusion, taking some kind of order.

Robles jumped over the trough and ran hard

around the house to the left with Urbina behind him. From out of the cut, Fernando started firing, towards the corral. Robles and Urbina shielded themselves behind an adobe well and saw the Sloan gang saddling up and spurring their horses out The five men raced northward on their fresh mounts, bullets singing past them and kicking up the ground about them.

They rode out of range as Robles watched helplessly. He then crossed the rear of the station and found the three bodies. One of them moved, turning slowly on its side. That was Lucero. The other two would never move. Lopez was unrecognizable, the .44 slug having taken off half his face.

Walking unsteadily to the wall, Robes collasped against its side. It had been a long time since his last combat, too long. Lucero was bleeding on the ground and he didn't have the will to do anything about it. He cursed Lucero for getting shot, for leaving him with no one to blame but himself. With a feeling even more sickening, Robles then realized that he could not leave it at this. They would come to him or he would have to go to them. He could feel the hate spreading through him, like a venom coursing through his veins.

6

Tolfane got up from the leather chair behind his desk and stepped towards Cajun.

"I can not impress upon you enough how important this is. At all times you must use restraint and cool-headed judgement when dealing with these men. What happened last night at Gallino Station is a perfect example of what I'm talking about. Those Mexicans may have had a perfectly good reason for going after the Sloan bunch, but they went about it all wrong. Not only did they mishandle the thing, the very fact that they went in shooting like that makes it inevitable that more violence is yet to come. There will be no end to it if this sort of thing keeps happening." He turned quickly to the door. "Oh yes, Jenkins, I'll be ready in just a minute."

Lafe Jenkins nodded in acknowledgement and leaned against the door jamb.

"So, in effect, Mr. Lee, plan of action is this—we guard all ranch property and recover all that is stolen in the most peaceable way possible. We already have had some success at this. Remember, Baehma's gang can't survive without stolen property and the more we frustrate them in this respect, the sooner the faction will break up and leave the area. And this applies to anyone else's property or safety in the region, including the Mexicans. We're all in on this together.''

Cajun told him he understood and would do his best to go along with what the rancher said.

"Very well, then, Jenkins here will ride out with you and show you around. Give you an idea of how things are done.''

Cajun walked out with Lafe to find his new black hitched next to the range detective's roan. The day's rest and the two solid nights' sleep had done Cajun good. He had recovered much of his strength, and his two wounds were itching—a sure sign they were on the heal. To complete the picture, Tolfane's cook had even patched up his serape where it had been ripped by the bullet. If nothing else, in the Tolfane ranch he had found a fine place to put the pieces back together.

Riding the pass through the broken field of rock to the rear of the house, Cajun and Lafe entered Tolfane's vast grazing land. Lafe led the way around the perimeter, explaining the ranch hands' routine and the rotation of the range detectives' watch and pointing out the most likely approaches to the area. Along the way, Cajun was introduced to fellow regulators Ray Pence, George Caldwell, Charley Benton, Clell Forrest, Heck Buel—and got a sidelong glance from Phin. They worked their way northward toward a deep basin surrounded by a ragged strip of ridges and winding draws.

"When they try coming in on us," Lafe said, "the stock can be split up and tucked into a few spots around here. They can stay penned in and be protected from any shooting. There's plenty of places like that around here. Don't think I got to know 'em all yet.''

Cajun scanned the area quickly. "You been getting any real trouble around here?"

"Once in a while we have kind of a run-in. Usually not too much. Last month, though, a couple of us got shot at from that wall over to the west. It was Phin, Clell and some other fella. The other fella got hit. Can't walk now."

"What did you do about it?"

"Wasn't much we could do. We were pretty sure it was either Amos Claibourne or Morgan Fleet, but we weren't sure which. Mr. Tolfane said we couldn't do anything without being certain."

"He's really serious about us holding back?"

"He means what he says. Phin was like to quit over that shooting but he ended up staying anyhow. Me, I don't care what the man wants to pay us for. That's his business. I just make sure no one gets the chance to take a crack at me."

They skirted the basin, turning into a pass that led to a level overlooking a gradual downward slope.

"From what I hear," said Lafe, "about that business in the cantina in Sloan, you'd best be doing a lot of making sure yourself."

Walking his black on to the level and turning towards the nearest beginning of the incline, Cajun caught sight of a man below—a lone man, crossing the flatlands on foot. Lafe followed the other man's gaze, then broke into a trot, slowing for the ride down the slope. Cajun caught up with him as they drew up next to the walking man.

Lafe smiled wryly. "Now what happened to you, Sam? You gambling away your horses these days?"

"You think it's funny, do ya?" Sam scratched

his chest furiously. "I didn't gamble it, if it's all the same to you. It was those boys in town. Billy Laughlin and his brother and a couple of others. I'd just gone in to get some supplies. They said they liked the color of my horse and they took it from me. Nothin' I could do—I didn't have no gun."

"Better for you that you didn't."

"Well, I'm gettin' one at my place and then I'm goin' back."

"You just go home and stay there, Sam." Turning to Cajun, Lafe said, "Looks like you're about to start earning your pay."

Sam chattered on about not needing anyone to fight for him while the two horsemen swung around and headed south for Sloan.

Lafe said, "Sam Gorton's got a small place just above Tolfane's. He's got a short ways to go and then he'll probably just stay there. He's only got the place because Tolfane lets him use some of his own land, so Sam is pretty used to letting Tolfane take care of him."

They rode in silence for a little more than a mile. When they reached the downward side of the Huecas, Lafe asked which ones of the Sloan gang Cajun had come across.

"There were the two Claibournes in the bar and the kid they called Tobey."

"He's no-account."

"I could see that. As for the others, I must have met a few in the mountains that night but it certainly wasn't no chance to get acquainted."

"This Billy Laughlin will be the one to watch this time. He's the best gun next to Baehma. He's also got more sense than the rest of the family."

Cajun gave him a half-smile. "That's a nice way

51

to put it. From what I've seen of them, I'm surprised that family knows how to keep walking.''

"They're crazy, all right. But that doesn't count 'em out. Josh Claibourne is tough. And so is Ave Laughlin. With that fella Amos, there's no tellin'. I'm not sure I'd like to go up against him. Levi Ruffner and Morgan Fleet are the two outsiders in the group and they have been around. As for the bunch of them put together, there ain't nothing they won't do that Johnny Baehma tells them and that's probably the worst of it.''

Cajun stored this information away, fixing a clearer picture in his mind of what the possibilities were. Glancing to his side, he made a quick study of this gunman with the firm, set lines in his face and the easy carriage in the saddle. Cajun figured that he probably had been in this line of work before. That could be another problem to get around.

Within sight of Sloan, they checked their rifles and hand guns. Walking their horses in a bit further, they could make out the four horses at the tie rail outside the cantina. There was no steeldust. Lafe led a circling route behind the cantina that kept them concealed, the back of the place being a blind wall. They reined in at the corral to the rear that held a half dozen horses. Lafe didn't see Sam Gorton's. He pushed his hat to the back of his head.

"They could have it at the post behind the old sheriff's office or by the shack or maybe even inside. Or they could have already sent someone with it to the Claibourne place just west of here. Or they could have it someplace we don't know about. We could look around, but they're bound to see us.

We wouldn't have any sort of edge if that happens."

Cajun turned toward the laughter coming from the cantina. "Go straight in?"

Lafe nodded and pulled the hat back down. "Back or front for you?"

The man in the serape liked the idea of a surprise. "The back."

They pulled their rifles and started off.

At the wooden door in back, Cajun could make out the voices inside. He stood waiting a short time; then all noise from the cantina stopped. Lafe was in.

"Hello, fellas. How's the whiskey today? Passable?"

"You pimping son of a bitch, what makes you think you can walk in here?"

Cajun shouldered through the door and sidestepped inside with his Spencer leveled.

The Laughlins were on either side of the front door—Jesse to the left, Billy at the bar to the right, neither of them more than a few feet from Lafe standing between them. Tobey was at the back end of the bar. Amos was standing by a table to the left and rear.

All eyes except Lafe's turned Cajun's way. Only Tobey had seen him the other night but they all knew him from the kid's description. Jesse and Amos looked rattled. Billy considered him with a penetrating glare.

Lafe said, "We've come about Sam Gorton's horse."

"What the hell about it?" said Jesse.

"We want to know where you put it after stealing it."

53

Jesse started telling him that they hadn't seen Gorton for days but before he finished Amos jerked suddenly towards Cajun.

"Damn you—"

He had his gun out when the room was suddenly filled with the blast of the Spencer. Amos's pistol spun from his hand. Before it hit the floor, Billy and Jesse threw down.

Lafe stepped once to the bar, rammed his rifle butt into Billy's face, wheeled fast, and sighted his barrel at Jesse's head before the man could clear leather.

Tobey watched open-mouthed, his hand poised tentatively near his holster. He turned to find the Spencer on him. Jesse, a little white around the eyes, dropped his gun back in place while Billy held his forehead and grabbed blindly for the top of the bar, blood seeping through his fingers.

Cajun was now very sure that Lafe had been in this line before.

Amos slumped down on the table, clutching his forearm. Not used to shooting to wing a man, Cajun had only grazed him.

"Now, about that horse," said Cajun.

"Jesus Christ," Jesse whined, "we was just funnin' the man. We wasn't going to keep it."

Billy steadied himself against the counter. "Shut up, Jesse, damn you!"

Lafe got a rag from behind the bar and handed it to Billy. Snatching it from his hand, Laughlin mopped some of the blood away. The rifle butt had slashed the skin but not much else. The sight was uglier than the actual damage.

The range detectives collected the guns, piled them on the floor in the middle of the room, and grouped the four men in a close line against the bar. Lafe stepped over to Jesse, staring him down for a moment before speaking.

"There something more you want to tell us about Sam's horse?"

Jesse darted a glance at his brother, then dropped his eyes to the floor.

Lafe crossed in front of the other three. "Now either you tell us and we get the horse and leave, or we keep you here until we find it for ourselves. Either way we'll get what we came for. It's just a matter of how you want to spend the afternoon, fellas. You want to stay bottled up in here? Maybe you want go at it again with us?"

No one answered. Lafe scanned the four faces, then indicated the door to Cajun. "Seems like one of us should go look."

Not relishing the idea of wasting the afternoon on a squatter's horse, Cajun hit upon an idea. Strolling down the line of men, he came to a stop with his back to Billy.

"Now I don't think anyone really wants that, Lafe. I don't think they want it any more than we do. Just think, what if Johnny Baehma were to come in now . . . wouldn't that look poorly?" He turned slowly to face Billy, locking stares. "Wouldn't it?"

Cajun watched the young man coolly, until a flicker of doubt shadowed Laughlin's eye.

"Wouldn't you say so, Billy?—him coming here and seeing you all like damn fools without your guns, them taken away by Tolfane men."

Billy spoke under his breath. "You got the drop on us."

"Us two?" said Cajun, "got the drop on you

four?"

The man in the serape turned away after a couple of moments and headed towards the door.

"It's by the shack," Billy blurted. "By the shack there, in the boarded-up sign shop."

Cajun had been right. A man who is second gun can be more touchy than others about how the top man sees him.

As Cajun went out the door, Billy added, "You can get it fast, right?"

The two range detectives exchanged a look.

Lafe said, "He's comin' that soon, huh?"

Cajun walked down the sun-baked street to the old sign shop. The slats across the jamb of the back door were loose and, with an unsteady creak, Cajun was able to push them in. The air inside the ten by twelve wood frame building was close and rank. Amongst the clutter of the signmaker's abandoned supplies and discarded junk was the old chestnut, snorting and shying slightly at the figure silhouetted against the sudden shaft of light. It was clear that the owner of the place had left suddenly, perhaps at the same time the sheriff's office was razed. It was also clear that the shop had become a hiding place. After calming the animal, Cajun looked the place over. Not finding any strong box or chest or anything else containing precious metal, he led the horse out, passed the shack on his way to the street, and decided to check the inside of that. No luck there either.

Further down the street, for the sake of being methodical, he considered looking to see what could be stashed in the rubble of the sheriff's office, when he saw the four outlaws being led out of the cantina, Lafe covering them from behind with their guns bound up in a blanket. Cajun kept on walking.

Finding the silver could well be a long process, but Cajun was willing to wait for his chance. It had been a long stretch since his last big stake in Fort Griffin and, to his mind, he certainly had as much right to this loot as anyone else in the region. Tolfane wanted the Sloan bunch made so frustrated that they would break up. That was fine. As soon as this pack got around to falling apart, something would be bound to come to the surface—hopefully, something very valuable.

Lafe went around to get the horses while Cajun kept an eye on the Sloan men. On returning, Lafe gave out a warning about future stealing and the two range detectives rode out with Sam's horse. Billy watched from under his brow, his jaw set hard.

Cajun and Lafe were two miles up the road from town when they saw the rider coming towards them from behind the shoulder of rock. Another quarter mile and Johnny Baehma was drawing up slow alongside them, his look shifting from the two men to the chestnut, saying nothing.

Lafe brought Sam's horse closer to the outlaw chief.

"Recognize this, Johnny?"

"No. Why should I?"

"It belongs to Sam Gorton. Some of your boys got a little mixed up and thought it was theirs. Maybe it'll be better if you tell them it should stay with Sam."

"Don't tell me about it, Jenkins. What they do is their business."

"Just an idea, Johnny."

Baehma's look moved to Cajun and stayed there. Lafe continued.

"You know that no matter what's taken, we're coming to take it back."

Still staring at Cajun, Johnny said, "I know who you are, mister."

"I've been hearing about you too," Cajun said.

"Tolfane paying you now?"

"That's right."

Baehma nodded slowly. "Claibournes are like kin to me. You ever come after me for anything, you better be ready to go to work."

"I'll remember that, Johnny."

Lafe had turned his roan to the north for the ride back to the ranch. Cajun stayed in place, toying with a reckless thought as he held Baehma's gaze. This time was as good as any to test the ground.

"I like the horse," he said to Baehma. "I used to race horses like that when I was a boy. It was the first kind I learned to ride. I'd sure like to have it."

"I ain't doing business with you. I never will"

"Like I said, I'm especially partial to it."

"No business."

Cajun spoke his words slowly. "Maybe when I come, it'll be just for the steeldust."

Baehma's green eyes flared, his lips tightened. Cajun looked at him for what seemed a long time. There was a ready malevolence to the outlaw's stare. That and something else.

Baehma said, "You're digging it for yourself now, mister."

Cajun swung around and rode off without answering.

Lafe glanced back as they pulled away to see Baehma still sitting on his horse, glowering at their backs. He then looked quizzically at the man beside him and shook his head.

The something else that Cajun thought he had seen was a brief play of hesitation in Baehma. That could have been either uncertainty or shrewdness. Cajun was going to have to take this man one step at a time.

7

They were all around the table at the Claibourne ranch that night. Josh had been brought out of his room and propped up in a chair. Though waning, the fever was still with him, but this was family business and he couldn't spend the time lying in his bed.

Amos hunched forward in his seat as he spoke.

"These are foreigners and heathens to boot. You see them wearing crosses and going to church and such, but that doesn't mean nothing a'tall. The Lord doesn't listen to them. He knows what they are really like. The way they act is proof of that. Nobody but godless men would attack us the way they did at Gallino Station. If Johnny hadn't of been there, we might of left this world that night. We must exact from them what is due."

"And there's that stranger," said Sol. "He's still around and, like Johnny says, workin' for Tolfane now."

Billy reached for the bottle and poured himself another shot, downing it in one gulp.

Jesse said, "What're we gonna do, Johnny?"

Baehma stopped pacing at the end of the table and grabbed the top of the chair Josh was sitting in.

"There can't be no more waiting. Ike and Aaron and Nick were killed three nights ago, the greasers shot up Gallino Station last night, and today Tolfane men came into the cantina."

Morgan Fleet snuffed his cigar on the table. "I got a look at a couple of those beaners last night. I think I recognized 'em. We could go out to their places tonight."

"We got to do this right," said Baehma. "We got to think about it. We got to think what the Old Man would've done."

The men at the table watched him, waiting for his next words. He looked off towards the blank wall before him, then turned away slowly and walked to the near window. When he walked out and saddled the steeldust, there were no questions asked and no explanations offered. The men at the table listened to him ride off, refilled their glasses and settled in for the wait.

Baehma might be away a half hour or an hour or maybe more. One time he'd been gone half the night. No one would go after him—there could be no hurrying these things. The Claibournes and the Laughlins always knew this and the outsiders had learned it quickly.

Occasionally Jesse would try to break the silence with stories of what he was going to do when they reached Red Rock this month, but no one led him on and the attempts at conversation fell flat. Too much was going wrong. All that mattered now was whatever Johnny came up with.

The bottle of whiskey was finished and another one started by the time Baehma returned. He strode through the door and, going to the head of the table, helped himself to a drink.

"Being at the Old Man's place," he said, "made me see all this much better."

Ave said, "Do we go out for 'em tonight?"

Baehma's brow lowered as he gave the man a considering look. "I know what you boys are thinking. You think we should go out and find those Mexicans and do to them what they tried to do to us. And maybe take the stranger too."

"That'd be a start," Ave muttered. Amos chimed in that the time had come.

"Well, that's not what we are going to do." Baehma moved along the length of the table, studying the perplexed faces turned his way. Unlike most of his decisions, this time Baehma would have to explain himself. "We've got to hurt them the best way we can. We might be able to round them all up and give them what they deserve and maybe we might not. But that's not the point. When I was out there in the hills I got to thinking what the Old Man would've done and then it come to me. What're we talking about here? Beaners, that's all. We don't have to go out gunning for them. They're not worth the trouble."

Voices rose in a jumble, protesting, asking what he could be meaning.

"We're not letting anyone get away with anything, don't you worry about that. I'm just saying we're not gunning for them. What we're going to do is slap 'em in the face and spit in their damn eye."

Baehma drank his whiskey until someone asked him how.

"We're going to rustle them for all they got. We'll take every bit of stock we can get a hand on."

The men looked at each other unsurely, saying nothing. Billy Laughlin broke the silence.

"What do we want that for, Johnny? Most of that Mex cattle ain't nothing but scraggly shits. What're we goin' to deal in that for?"

Amos twisted around in his chair, his gaze flicking quickly from his cousin to Johnny Baehma, desperately trying to make sense of this.

"That's just part of it," Johnny said.

"What about the stranger?" asked Sol, half rising. "What about what happened to Ike and Nick and Aaron?"

"One thing at a time. First we rustle those bastards. You want to go out for blood—what's that going to get us? There's no business in that. And we got more here than just some greasers gone out of line. If we're going to keep on around here, we're going to have to be able to take what we want, no matter who tries to stop us."

Baehma circled the table and told them what they were going to do the next day. The men now let him speak without interruption. First Billy, then Josh came around to his thinking and said as much. The others were not far behind. When Baehma ended his talk, Amos was rocking slightly back and forth, his eyes dilated and dark.

"Of course," Baehma added, "like Sol was saying, this still leaves the stranger. But we'll leave him for now. I'll take care of that when the time comes."

"That's if nobody else beats you to it."

It was Billy speaking. Baehma looked at him with some suspicion, then laughed gruffly. He poured another round for the two of them.

"We'll see, Billy. We'll see."

Amos rose to his feet, shaking a first. "Vengeance is ours." He pounded the table top and cackled fitfully.

Tolfane and his wife had left the porch and gone inside a half hour before. Not seeing any of the servants about the house or any of the ranch hands outside, Cajun circled behind one of the bunkhouses and made for the corral holding his black. He could walk the animal out of the flat and into the hills and then ride on without attracting any attention.

Gallino Station would be his next stop. Since the Sloan bunch was supposed to often pass through and stay on there, Cajun counted on a fair chance of learning something from its owner. The silver may have been taken out of Sloan and brought south.

At the end of the bunkhouse, Cajun paused to allow his eyes to fully adjust to the darkness. He waited for a shuffling sound from inside to die down and, walking quickly but without haste, headed for the corral. This early on, he wasn't about to take any chances on giving himself away. If he was seen, there would be no reason to think anything unusual about him. He had the black hitched to the outside of the railing, ready to be led away. Some twenty feet short of the corral, Cajun saw her.

She must have left the house while he was checking on the ranch hands. Cajun stopped and watched Mrs. Tolfane walk towards him from the stand of cottonwood past the last corral, her shawl waving slowly in the breeze as she drew herself together against the cooling night air. Cajun had only caught brief glimpses of her before, usually from a distance, and when she came close he found she lived up to what he had expected.

She was a woman of average height who appeared much taller because of a long-looking, lithe figure. In the pale light her auburn hair, now bobbed loosely in the back, still picked up an occasional reddish shine. She approached Cajun smiling faintly, her round brown eyes seeming instantly familiar. She was much younger than Tolfane.

They exchanged good evenings.

"What a beautiful night," she said. "I love so much to walk out here in the evening on my own, but Mr. Tolfane tells me I shouldn't. He says a lady should never go out without an escort at this time. Don't you think he's silly?"

"He may have a point."

"Oh, perhaps."

Her words were clearly shaped and rounded by some finishing school back east. Cajun thought the manner was a bit overdone, but her voice was silky enough and her gestures graceful enough to carry it off well.

"I don't want to be a bother, but would you be so kind as to walk with me back to the house? Mr. Tolfane will scold me if he sees me coming back alone. You don't mind, do you?"

Cajun agreed and tried to imagine Tolfane liking the idea of her walking with a hired gun.

"I hope they settle all the trouble around here soon. I just can't go anywhere anymore what with these outlaws running wild through the region. Before everything became so horrid, Mr. Tolfane and I used to go for rides in the evening on the buckboard, but things being as terrible as they are, we wouldn't even think of it. Isn't it horrible? I simply get so bored sometimes.''

She continued on with such matters as they neared the front porch, relating these troubles as if they were of the most earnest and intimate concern. At one point Cajun was almost taken in enough to think that they were. For this reason, he didn't notice the shadowed figure against the side of the house.

After watching her go in the front door, Cajun scanned the area between the house and the corral. He could still make it to his horse, sneak off, and be back well before morning. He retraced his steps silently, reaching the railing and taking the reins before hearing the voice from behind.

"Kind of early to take your four o'clock shift, ain't it?"

Cajun turned to see the man standing a short piece away.

"There something you want to say to me, Phin?"

Phin walked closer, his hands clasped around the front of his gun belt. "I was just sayin' it's a hell of a time for you to be starting off for somewhere.''

"I don't recall saying I was going anywhere.''

"Well, that's good, Cajun. With this job we need all the sleep we can grab. Just one fella who don't take the job serious makes it worse for the rest of us. You'd best sit tight and just do what you're told.''

Cajun loosened the saddle, swung it off, and led the black to the entrance to the corral. When it was inside, he met Phin's stare.

Cajun said, "You don't plan on doing anything but talking, Phin, so just drop it right now.''

Cajun started for the bunkhouse, Phin having

no reply until he'd gone a few steps further.

"One more thing, Cajun. Just watch who you go talking to here."

"Who would you be talking about?"

"You know what I mean."

Cajun considered the man's tightly wound face, didn't think him worth the time, and continued on his way. He would leave it for tonight and make it to Gallino Station tomorrow. He went to sleep in his bunk that night wanting to disregard Phin's warning as the thoughtless words of a swaggerer.

8

Robles finished his coffee, rinsed the cup in the basin and stood by the window, wondering what he could do with himself. He settled on smoking his pipe, hoping that would occupy him until the boy came in to start work. Robles' frame house was not large, but with his wife, Luisa, and the children gone it seemed to be made of great empty spaces—just as his time had become mercilessly slow.

Like his neighbors, Robles had sent away the women and the little ones in his family after the disaster at Gallino Station. That the Sloan gang would strike back was a certainty and Robles for one could not afford to give them a second chance against his family.

He lit the pipe, turning towards the mirror over the bureau and searching the face before him. It was a round, well-formed face, scored with deep lines about the mouth and burnished by many years of work out in a harsh land. Robles examined the skin now sunken below his eyes. He tried to discover in this image the reason why he had turned into such a weak, shuddering man. He had fought in the Indian Wars and then went on to build a home and a living out of nothing. Now he felt helpless as soon as the women in the house were gone. Another man would have laid it all to the work of the desperados in the area, but Robles couldn't leave it at that. He still had to live with himself.

He was roused from his thoughts by the clatter of hoofs outside. That would be the boy. Robles put out his smoke, picked up his hat and walked out to his pinto hitched in front. Outside, the sight of the rider made him stop short.

It was Tomas all right, but he was closing in on the house from the ridge at a thundering gallop. The boy pulled up roughly by the hitching rail, panting breathlessly as he steadied his animal.

"What is it, Tomas? What is it?"

The strain on the boy's sweaty face increased as he worked for the breath to speak. "Felipe is shot!" he gasped. "The cattle—they're taking all the cattle!"

Robles strode forward, and grabbed the pommel on the boy's saddle. He thought he would have something to say, some question to ask. Wheeling suddenly, he ran into the house for his Henry and his loads, came back, swung up onto the pinto and, after briefly fighting down the churning sickness in his stomach, beat the flanks of the animal and took off for the ridge.

On the other side of the ridge was the grazing land he shared with the Lucero family. Felipe Lucero had been watching the herd through the early hours of the morning. He had turned seventeen two months before. Robles' mind spun between fury and fear as he reached to bottom of the slope and prodded his horse up the rocky incline. He looked back to see if Tomas was behind him, the first time he had thought to do so; then, finding the boy close to his rear, Robles walked the pinto into the pass and broke into a gallop again. A sudden wave of caution brought him up short. He swung around to climb up the winding path that would lead him to higher ground. From there he could see what was going on across the flats before plunging in. He spurred the horse to the top, circled about a pinnacle and reached his spot.

The cattle were rushing along the line of the arroyo, spurned on by four riders, already about a mile off. Down below was Felipe, stretched out on the ground, a hand groping aimlessly. Robles and Tomas came down the incline and raced to his side. Scrambling down off the saddle, Robles dropped to the boy's side, finding the bullet hole just above the left hip. He probably could live if someone could take care of him.

A new cluster of horse hoofs came from across the flat. Two riders were coming from the Lucero ranch. Robles turned to Tomas.

"You stay here. Do what you can for Felipe."

He mounted the pinto, shot a glance back at the boy on the ground and charged off to meet the other two horsemen.

The herd was now turned, headed to the north. Robles joined Urbina and Camilo Lucero along the arroyo. They splashed across the shallow bed and beat their animals toward the rear of the herd, looking small on the dust-swirled horizon.

With beads of sweat on his upper lip, Anson let his eyes wander once again towards the front window, as if looking for someone. Cajun couldn't tell if that look was hopeful or afraid. He reached across the table and brought back the man's attention by tilting the bottle and refilling the glass.

"Anyone supposed to be coming, Joe?"

"No," Anson replied more forcefully than necessary. "No, there ain't nobody comin'. Not that I know of."

"Well, then, you can talk all you want."

Running his fingers around the glass, Anson watched the play of light on the surface of the cloudy liquid with eyes flecked with red. "I don't know that I should."

Cajun leaned back in his chair and scrutinized the station owner. "If that's the way it is, Joe, all I can say is this. I'm going to ask you just so long—then, that's it."

Anson took a gulp of the mescal and looked at the man in the serape, his thick featured face plainly showing he didn't understand.

"This is what I'm telling you, Joe. I work for Tolfane. You know that. And I'm looking for stolen goods. You know that too. What you don't know, is that Mr. Tolfane has made a deal with the governor. By next month there's going to be a posse of U.S. Marshals coming down here to clean up this place. Now these men are a rough sort. They are going to take care of everybody. And if they hear that you flat refused to help out on this here, they're going to come after you too."

Cajun sat quietly to let this sink in. Anson's jaw had dropped. He quickly finished his drink and said that he hadn't heard anything about that.

"Most people don't know." Cajun gestured to Anson's hand on the glass. "You said before that you lost those two fingers because of the Sloan bunch. Seems to me like you're better off keeping with us."

Anson mulled this over. He started nodding his head in mute agreement, then spread his hands out, palms up, in a gesture of helplessness.

"I don't know what to tell you. I don't know nothing. They don't hide things here."

"You haven't seen them stash anything away here the last couple of days?"

"No, I swear."

Cajun refilled the glass. He thought the station owner looked drunk and broken down enough to be telling the truth. "Maybe you can still help me anyway, Joe."

"How?"

"The Sloan boys were here two days ago, right? That night they got shot at. Tell me exactly who was here and when they came and where they were coming from."

Anson groped in his mind for the details of that day and in bits and pieces came up with the sequence of events. He told about Amos, Sol, and Morgan Fleet coming in during the afternoon, most likely coming from Sloan, and Jesse joining them soon after, coming from the Laughlin ranch. They didn't bring anything with them nor did they mention anything about stolen goods. Johnny Baehma rode in just before dark. The others were surprised to see him.

"Where was he coming from, you remember?"

Working his mouth thoughtfully, Anson said, "I think it was from the west. Yeah, that's it. From the west and a bit to the north." He smiled at Cajun with satisfaction.

"And the others didn't know he was coming?"

"Yeah, that's right. I remember Jesse saying he thought Johnny was going to be in Sloan."

"Any of them know where he had been?"

"I don't think so. Don't think any of them asked either. They never seem to ask what he's been up to. Like they're not supposed to."

Cajun had him go over the story once more to see if it came out the same and then got up to leave. Anson didn't have anything more for him and it was getting close to noon. If he didn't want to rouse any suspicion, he'd best be getting back to the Tolfane place. He and Lafe had gone out that morning to escort two groups of stray cattle back to their owners' ranches. Lafe was probably well on his way back by now.

Anson finished the rest of the bottle and, pushing himself to a standing position, staggered towards the back room, changed his mind half-way and steered himself to a nearby bench.

"Never knew," he slurred, "that I would know enough for people to be asking me about things."

"Well, keep your eyes and ears open and they'll ask you more. And there might be something in it for you."

Cajun was headed for the door when the station owner said, "Yeah, that's what the feller yesterday said."

Cajun stopped and walked back a couple of paces. "What feller is this?"

"Oh, I don' know. This feller."

"What was he asking you?"

Anson's eyelids drooped as he slumped backwards. "The same thing. The same thing you were. Looking for stolen goods."

"Who was it, Joe? Did you know him?"

Anson curled up on the bench and said he didn't.

"What did he look like?"

"I don' remember. He got me so stinking."

"Notice anything about him?"

Anson spoke in a soft groan. "I don' remember. Said he worked for Tolfane—had dark hair—"

"Anything else? Joe. Joe."

He moved quickly to the bench and shook Anson's arm, but the man was already out, snoring deeply.

George Caldwell and Heck Buel spent the morning along the northern ridges, checking on some unfamiliar tracks spotted along the basin. Skirting the western perimeter as the primary sentries were Phin and Clell Forrest. Ray Pence and Charley Benton were ranging toward the east. It was Pence who first picked up the low rumbling sound, differentiating it from the drone of the Tolfane stock.

Casting his gaze quickly from side to side, he tried locating the source of the noise. The sound grew and, as Benton first heard it, Pence whirled around to see a herd storming along the top of the west wall, pounding dangerously close to the hundred foot drop. He muttered, "What the hell—?"

He then got the answer to his unfinished question.

He saw four riders driving the herd. One of them wore an bright red sash to protect his face from the churning dust. Pence knew that that sash concealed the face of Billy Laughlin.

The two range detectives reined their horses around and rode hard for the wall of rock. They cut down their pace while weaving through the Tolfane stock so as not to spook them. At the base of the wall, Phin and Forrest couldn't make out what was going on overhead, but Caldwell and Buel had a clear view and were already on their way. The six men clustered together while the cowhands tried distracting the cattle from the excitement.

"Laughlin's got some cattle," said Pence.

Phin craned his head toward the wild run above. "They're bringing 'em here?" he asked incredulously.

Turning to the south, Pence saw a new clutch of riders coming on fast from the base of the Huecas. "Maybe that's their reason."

"Looks like Mex riders," said Benton.

"Looks the same to me. And looks like we can't stay here talkin'."

Acting as top man with Lafe gone, Pence told Forrest and Caldwell to stay behind. He led the other three at a gallop toward the north end of the wall.

They worked a crooked path that inclined slowly, heading toward the point where the sloping edge of the basin met the elevated flat that ran along the top of the wall.

From a concealed pocket on the jagged opposite side of the basin, a head rose into the open, taking an unobstructed view of the range detectives scaling the irregular incline. The man watched as they topped their path and clattered on the flat. He judged they were already a good mile and a half to the rear of the stolen herd, not much better than the Mexicans. Figuring on some confusion when the cattle owners and the Tolfane men drew abreast, the distance for the rustlers would then lengthen; and by the time the cattle were herded west into the canyon beyond Copper Ridge, the stock could be slowed to an easier pace and run through the last stretch south without any interference.

When he saw the pursuers recede a safe distance away, Johnny Baehma turned from his lookout position to face the four men behind him.

"Now," was all he said.

Baehma led the steeldust into a winding draw, with Amos, Sol, Morgan and Ave leading their own behind him. They stayed on foot for about fifty yards, coming to a hollow of shale that rose on the far side to a pair of rounded hills. On the other side of that was the grazing land.

With the clamor from above well past them, the ranch hands now had the stock settled again. There were five of them that day, working 150 head. Caldwell and Clell Forrest were on either side. Forrest was angling toward the east for a look at the approach through the wash when the volley of fire shattered the newfound quiet.

The horse under Caldwell buckled and wrenched to the ground. One of the cowhands took a slug in the thigh. Baehma and Sol rode down one of the twin hills bordering on the north, virtually on top of the herd. Ave and Amos rattled down the other and circled to the other side while Morgan Fleet levered away with his Winchester from the top.

The herd became a tangled eddy of frightened beasts. One of the cowboys tried to steer a leader, and got enmeshed in a fast milling pack. Forrest swung around to a hail of fire from Baehma and Sol and lurched for the cover of a boulder, spilling out of the saddle and yanking his carbine out at the same time.

Caldwell was pinned under the weight of his

horse. He clawed and squirmed his way out as the cattle swerved to his side. Scrambling to a shoulder of rock, he flattened himself on the ground and drew his six-shooter. On the other side, Forrest had set himself, positioning himself for a clear shot. Then the herd moved.

The Sloan men spooked them in one direction and the 150 head became one mass, rushing madly to the south. The cowhands were on the wrong side, in front of their path, and had to get out of the way in a hurry. The cowboys trapped in the middle simply dropped from sight. The two range detectives tried sighting on the rustlers, but Baehma charged by with both Smith & Wessons blasting, the reins clenched in his teeth, making Forrest hug the side of the boulder while the spread of the cattle on the other side drove Caldwell back to further cover.

In a matter of seconds, the frenzied procession was past, on its way to the gap in the broken field. Forrest now had a clear line on one of the riders to the rear. He ran forward, slammed the carbine to his shoulder and then, with the electric realization that he had made himself an open target, spun to his left and dove for a mound that shielded him from the twin rounded hills. He landed sliding on the ground, casting a glance to the hill on the right, the perch for Morgan Fleet's rifle work.

The hill was empty.

Forrest frantically ran his eye across the surrounding land. He crawled toward a line of rock. To his side, from behind the hill, came the hoof beats. Forrest turned in time to see Fleet bearing down on him, thirty feet away, the smoke pouring from his Colt. Two more shots came after the first and they both crashed through Forrest around his mid-section. He crumpled down and writhed briefly—then lay still.

Caldwell cut loose as Morgan Fleet sped across the other side of the open, but his handgun couldn't cover the distance. The rustler rode off to catch up with the rest. Left in the otherwise empty grazing spread was a gunned down range detective, one wounded cowboy, and three others to pick up the cowboy who'd been trampled to pulp on the ground.

9

Not having the time to rouse Anson into any sort of speaking condition, Cajun Lee left Gallino Station for the Tolfane ranch. He started to the west and came to the road leading to Sloan. He had gone five miles when he saw the rider to his left, too distant to make out clearly. The horseman was heading south, riding slowly along the base of the craggy range beyond him, occasionally shifting to the side, then returning to his main path. Further on, Cajun thought he recognized the rider's bearing and handling of the horse. Breaking into a trot, he veered off the road to get a better look and was soon able to see that it was Lafe after all. He prodded the black into a faster gait, crossing an alluvial fan, and in a few moments was drawing up to Jenkins' side.

Lafe's eyes were on the hard packed earth. "Thought you'd be back by now, Cajun."

The man in the serape walked his black alongside and followed Lafe's intent look. He made out the sign—five shod horses, going north.

Lafe said, "Came across this on my way back from the Bittner ranch. First spotted it by Sloan. It was clear enough they were headed toward Tolfane's so I backtracked to here to see if my guess was right about who they belong to."

Looking ahead as far as he could make out the sign, Cajun saw the line drifting to the right, south and west.

"That'd make it the Laughlin place, right?"

Lafe turned to him, nodding. "You're right."

They reined to a stop, studying the line of trail a moment more.

"Don't know what they're up to," said Lafe, "but we got six of our own still back there, which should take care of that end. Might not be a bad idea to keep on to the Laughlins and wait."

They considered the points for surprising the boys on their home ground. As they talked they heard low, dense rumbling off to the north. The noise grew and, as one, the two men made their animals bolt toward the mountains, circling about a shoulder of rock and climbing up to higher cover.

They dismounted and settled in along a ledge. They saw the herd in the distance, driven in their direction. It didn't take long for them to spot the stock as Tolfane's and make out the riders as Sloan men. The cattle were moving fast, but not as furiously as before. They would be abreast of the two range detectives in a couple of moments, the time Cajun and Lafe needed to determine their ploy.

"We could let them by," Lafe said. "Follow from a distance and find the hideout."

"They're going to cover their tracks somewhere along the way. We could lose them if we play it too safe."

"And if we stick too close, the five of them could trap us."

Cajun crept to the horses, pulled out his Spencer and Lafe's Winchester, and hurried back.

"We scare them a little," he said, "and they might make a mistake. Something we could follow."

Lafe lined up the Winchester along the ledge and turned to Cajun with a quiet smile. "You been in this business before?"

Cajun shot him a sly glance as he sighted on the Spencer. "Let's just say I know the mind of a rustler."

Lafe's smile broadened.

The herd rolled towards them. The ledge was almost fifty yards above the flat, the herd about twenty-five feet from the base of the range. The range detectives could now recognize the five riders—Baehma, Fleet, Amos, Sol, and Ave.

Lafe said, "Let a couple go by, Cajun. We want to find the hideout." His smile then disappeared and he set himself for the shot. The herd came alongside. The Winchester cracked first.

Ave grabbed his left arm, but didn't slow. Only a flesh wound. The Spencer bucked and Sol's shoulder jerked forward. The cattle lurched ahead into a new pace, spooked again and picked up speed. Baehma spurred his animal on, the steeldust immediately breaking into a hard gallop, the outlaw chief shifting in the saddle, raking the mountains for the source of the gunfire. Bullets cut the air around the rustlers. They yelled and shot off their guns, driving the animals faster. Huge clouds of dust rose and the Sloan men became virtually hidden.

With the dust engulfing their targets, Cajun and Lafe raised their fire to just above the herd, taking care not to hit any of the stock. They continued pumping lead to keep the rustlers on edge, chasing them across the flat. The cattle were turned in a long curve and sent around a slab of rock into an opening in the range between an escarpment and a bank of stone, where they angled out of view. Cajun replaced the spent tube in the stock of the Spencer. The range detectives allowed the outlaws time to be on their way, then went for their horses and started along the side of the rise.

At the beginning of the ravine, Baehma reined the steeldust to a slow stop, letting the cattle stream by. The close steep walls ahead bunched the herd and forced them to cut down on their run. Baehma called to Sol Claibourne.

"How badly are you?"

On the opposite side of the stock, Sol pulled his horse into a walk. With effort he corrected his slump and brought up the drilled shoulder. "I'll make it," he rasped.

Amos was at the lead, guiding the beasts along the narrow floor. Baehma was able to take some satisfaction in that. The touched man would be best off up there and out of the way.

The outlaw chief concentrated his gaze on their back-track, now mostly blocked, as if trying to divine what was on the other side. Ave Laughlin and Morgan Fleet drew up alongside him.

Baehma said, "You two slip back. Give us some time. We won't need much."

Without answering, the two men about-faced and rode off. They turned left up the slope and disappeared behind a jutting formation.

Cajun and Lafe led their horses at first, wanting to keep close to the ground until they were sure of the trail ahead. They stayed the same distance up the rise and moved deliberately over the flayed, stubbled ground, sticking to the low rim of an overhanging shelf. The first shot came from above. It bounced whining off the shelf. A second and third came from ahead, one grazing the roan's flank.

The range detectives yanked their horses, bringing them under the cover of the shelf. They loose-tied them to a stunted shrub and flattened to the ground, their rifles poised.

Lafe scrambled toward a boulder a few feet ahead, drawing fire from the sniper across from them. Crouched with his back to the boulder, he said, "The one above's no use as long as we stick here." The upground rifleman opened up again, spraying the top of the shelf. "You see the other?"

Cajun ducked back fast as bullets kicked dust in front of him. He cleared his eyes. "He's across the hollow, down behind some of those rocks."

They squeezed their words into the gaps in the barrage.

"You keep your eye on him, Cajun. He's yours."

"How you want to get up there for the other?"

"I'll go out first. You'll cover. I'll keep 'em busy when you go."

They both levered their rifles. The ground dipped slightly behind Cajun. The man in the serape snaked back, shifted over towards Lafe, slid back up around a yard, and set himself next to the other range detective, his Spencer lined up with the outside edge of the boulder, resting on the ground.

Lafe waited out the end of the volley. With the first space of quiet, he braced and sprang out into the open. Cajun's right hand was a blur as he pelted the rifleman's position across the hollow.

The Sloan man stayed down. Lafe hurtled for the deep cut across the path. Rifle fire poured down from above. Lafe spun down behind the cover while bullets gouged the ground behind him. He flushed himself against the side of the cut, listening to the fire persist with a vengeance, glancing to his left at the craggy slope along the forward path.

Cajun edged to the side of the boulder and slipped in a new cartridge cylinder. From the cut, Lafe would be able to open up on both snipers. Just as easily, though, he could be pinned down by them. Cajun eyed the cut for some kind of sign, but Lafe stayed out of sight. The man in the serape sent two shots across the hollow to keep the rifleman honest, and waited some more. Then his eyes swerved up the path. Some fifteen feet forward of the cut, Lafe had come to a new position, now wedged between two rocks, blazing away at the shooter above the shelf. Immediately, the man on the other side of the hollow swung his fire to Lafe. Cajun seized the opportunity.

He dashed up the path, clearing the shelf before he became the target. Moving to his right, he got himself to cover from above a spire; then he pivoted suddenly, snapped two shots at the gun ahead, and vaulted and rolled in a cat-like turn behind a shoulder on the uphill side.

Further along the path, on the other side of the shoulder, he could see a shallow gully that twisted towards the top of the ridge. Someone could belly up that and pick a way around the uphill gun. Diagonally across the path, sloping down, was a sharply cut sweep of ground giving cover for a run around the hollow. Cajun turned to Lafe on the other side of the path. The range detective stopped

84

his fire, pointed to himself, and waved across to the uphill side.

Cajun watched as Lafe squeezed three shots up the rise and then, squatting low, sprinted across in a crouch. Cajun fired across the hollow. Lafe scrambled to the gully, flopped against its side, and sent a spray of bullets towards the ridge. Cajun fired once more and rushed across the path to the rocks Lafe had abandoned. He rolled down the slope, braked himself by a scalloped rise, and, bounding to his feet, started a weaving path around the hollow.

The seven riders reined to a stop well before the beginning of the draw. The sides were steep and the floor narrow; up ahead they could see where it turned sharply to the left. The Sloan men could easily pick a spot on the other side of that turn for an ambush, nesting themselves among the dry rills along the sides.

Ray Pence said, "Go on ahead, Charley. Look it over."

Benton dismounted, pulled his carbine and entered the draw, working slowly along one side, studying the markings on the floor.

Pence watched with a new wave of weariness as Benton made his way along the sun-baked earth. He narrowed his eyes against the glare of the sun and straightened his back, picking his sweat-drenched shirt away from his skin. Since passing forty, this sort of work drained him more than he cared to admit. Especially so, he considered bitterly, when you take on extra men who you can't be sure are reliable.

He regarded the three Mexicans sitting on their

horses, showing no expression. He decided to try once more with the one who had talked for them before. "You don't have to keep on with us, you know. We can take it from here. With the kind of lead they got on us, all we're hoping on now is trailing them to their hideaway."

Robles turned to Camilo Lucero and Urbina, getting quick looks in return. "We will go on," he said, looking at Pence out of the corner of his eye.

"Damn lot of help you'll be," Phin muttered. Then, more directly: "Gallino Station your idea of taking care of your affairs?"

Pence turned to him and growled, "Leave it, Phin." As bad as riding with the Mexicans might turn out to be, Phin had a knack for making it worse.

Benton came back into view from behind the turn. He returned to the others at a jog.

"What's up, Charley?"

"Something, not bushwacking though."

"What?"

Benton said he'd show them. He mounted and led them into the draw. Once around the turn, they all stopped.

Six dead cattle were on the ground. The rope was still around their necks where they had been strung together and held in place. In that way, none of them would bolt when the Sloan men began shooting them down. They had all dropped in a pile, now a festering, fly-ridden barrier.

Pence scanned the sides of the draw with little hope. On both sides, the ground topped off in a narrow bevel, then climbed up to high bluffs. If they doubled back and circled around, their route would be too roundabout to be worthwhile. It might even take longer than clearing their way here.

Robles moved up alongside Pence, his face drawn tight as he glared at his dead stock.

"This enough for you?" said Pence.

Robles swung down, followed by Lucero and Urbina. The three of them took hold of one of the animals and began pulling, dragging it off by inches. Pence dismounted to pitch in, knowing that the chase was lost. If they hadn't been able to hear the Sloan men killing the cattle, they were too far behind already.

Beyond the ravine was a ride through a cluster of hills, and on the other side of that was Spider Pass, a forked path through a sheer-faced wall. Baehma, Amos, and Sol ran the Tolfane stock around the last hill and, reaching the wall, turned the cattle down the left route. To the side, Josh Claibourne steadied his horse against the raucous parade.

His wounded hip left him weak and kept him from moving too fast, but he was fit enough for the job today. He watched the herd pass and rumble down the left, then stooped to pick up the tied bundle of branches. Starting in a fan-like pattern about the opening to the pass, he swept the ground with the bundle, working his way inward. The ground was hard packed and pure rock layer in spots, leaving little substance for tracks. In a few minutes there was no sign of the herd's entrance into the fork.

Josh took his horses by the reins and, leading him down the left path, began to cover the rest of the sign.

Halfway around the hollow, Cajun ducked below a volley of fire and peered around the boulder to see the sniper dropping back. It was Morgan Fleet. The outlaw triggered two more shots, then skittered down out of sight behind a sharply turned slope.

Cajun ran for his next cover, where he crouched behind a mound. Fleet, lifting himself over the top of the slope, fired to keep him low. Cajun drove him back with a quick flurry of .56 slugs and searched ahead for his next dash—but stopped himself with a sudden realization at the back of his mind.

The firing had stopped from above.

Cajun swung around, backing against the mound, his eyes tracking the land towards the ridge. Lafe appeared from behind a comb-like formation and saw Cajun turn to him. He signaled toward the ravine at the south end of the range. The other gun had made off. Lafe worked down the slope towards the horses.

Covering for himself with two shots in Fleet's direction, Cajun ran bent-kneed for his next cover, circled to his left, and bellied to the top of the downward slope, thirty feet from where he'd seen the outlaw last. At the bottom of the incline, running behind a flat-faced hill, was Morgan Fleet. Before he made any progress downward, Cajun heard the clatter of hoofs galloping away.

Cajun turned back, meeting Lafe half-way as the range detective brought over the horses.

"They got their horses," Cajun said.

The two men swung aboard, cantered to the slope. At its base they picked up the trail. The two Sloan men had ridden to the ravine, where the herd had entered, and then continued on west in a direction of their own. The range detectives took the ravine. Knowing that Baehma had no more men to spare for sniper-work, they drove their horses hard, not bothering with scouting ahead. They took the winding path through the hills, reached Spider Pass, and drew up short.

Dismounting, Lafe paced about the smooth ground. He took off his hat, wiped his brow and, letting out a pained sigh, smacked the hat against his thigh.

"We're done," he said.

Cajun walked his black to the fork, went down the right path a few yards, retraced his steps, and then did the same down the left.

Returning to Lafe, he said, "What're we waiting for?"

"No use."

"What're you talking about? They only had two ways to go."

Lafe shook his head dejectedly and replaced his hat, pulling it down with a jerk. "This here's Spider Pass. No way you could know about it yet, but there ain't no way we're finding them now. It's just two paths out here, but you go in there, there's a whole mess of passes leading off. All sorts of ways they could have taken. We could ride around in there for hours and wouldn't be doing any damn good at all. Besides that, they could have a good man with a rifle on top somewhere, just in case."

Cajun looked off into the pass. What at first had looked like a fairly simple task of putting the screws on a band of low-grade crooks was now suddenly turned into something as tangled as the web of passes he was trying to picture.

"What now, Lafe?"

Lafe led his roan around and faced it to the north. "Looks like we have our work cut out for us." After saddling, he added, "When these boys are on their home ground, they are hard to beat."

10

He looked out of place in the bunkhouse. The range detectives had seen him in there only once before, when Tracey had been crippled by the shot from the wall, but even if Tolfane had passed through the place twice a day his presence there still would take some adjusting to. The swept back silver hair, the fine suit and brocaded vest and the stately walk, would never jibe with the dark slat-board walls and the tangy smell of men living together.

Pausing in his talk, Tolfane paced deliberately down the aisle running the length of the bunkhouse, his thin eyebrows bunched together in troubled thought. The men watched from their bunks as their employer stopped before the empty bed used by Clell Forrest.

Still gazing at the bed, he said, "I know you all realize the seriousness of what happened yesterday. Not only were my cattle rustled, but so were those of my Mexican neighbors. And one of those men was severely wounded—another horrible addition to the casualties we suffered."

He turned suddenly to face the group, his jaw now set firm. "And as tragic as all of this is on the face of it, the further consequences are even worse. These men have struck like lightning and in so doing have established themselves as virtual masters of the region. Any respect we can command with the neighboring ranches, both Anglo and Mexican, is drastically damaged. As for your way of handling the trouble yesterday, I think I'll have to reserve judgement."

He stepped down the line, looking unflinchingly from face to face. Cajun glanced about to see how the other detectives met this look. Phin and Caldwell were challenging, Ray Pence seemed almost relieved. The other three seemed to be reserving their own judgement.

"I hired you all in the belief that you were capable and I'm willing to continue in that belief. I do this partly because I am not as experienced as you in these matters and partly because, perhaps, I have not done everything right myself."

Tolfane toyed with the gold chain attached to his watch, then, in correcting the nervous gesture, clasped his hands together, wringing them slowly instead.

"Until now, I have tried to conduct this law and order effort in the most peaceable manner possible. I have urged you to use force only as much as was needed to bring a violent situation under control." He waved a hand to the side, as if brushing something away. "Perhaps, in dealing with men as desperate as these, that was my mistake."

The rancher's black eyes stared off absently as he reconsidered his thoughts. In another moment he broke off the reverie and stepped over to the row of hooks by the door where he collected his tan straw hat.

"You naturally know that all your effort has to be directed toward retrieving the stolen stock. How you go about it is something I will leave up to you. But I have one more thing to say: from now on you are all authorized by me to meet any show of force with any action you deem appropriate. Too much has been done for me to be able to afford the luxury of being civilized. Violence will be met with violence.''

The ride up the western slope took close to a half hour. Heck Buel prodded his horse up the last rise and reined in on the top flat, heaving for a breath of the thin, hell-hot air. Swinging off and leaving his animal ground-hitched for a deserved rest, he yanked out the carbine from the saddle sheath, crossed leisurely to the rim, and looked down the seventy-five foot drop to the bottom of Spider Pass.

Lafe acknowledged the signal from his man on top. He turned to the rest of his men. ''All clear from above. Phin, you and Caldwell take the left pass. Ray, you take the right with Charley. Work out the lead-offs as you go along.''

The four men got back on their mounts and rode off as they'd been told. Squinting against the harsh light, Cajun watched them go, running a thumb along the bottom of his moustache.

''Think it'll do much good?''

''Might,'' Lafe said. ''We got four working on it at once and another to make sure no one tries any business from the top. They could come up with something. At least it'll give us some better idea of what the possibilities are.''

Cajun let out a slow breath. ''You think as little of it as I do?''

''We have to try all the obvious things first. After this, we'll ask around at the other ranches in the area to see if anyone saw anything or spotted any new sign. Why, what you think of it?''

''I like doing things a bit more straight-away.''

''That's what I thought. Which is why I kept you out here. What's your thinking?''

''I figure we should get a hold of a couple of those Sloan boys and see if we can shake something out of them. They're the ones that know.''

''You think they'll just tell us like that?''

''Not really. But we may do something else. If they can trade all this stock off, they're going to have a lot of money coming their way. We talk to the right fellas in the right way, we could get them just a bit suspicious, get them thinking how much Baehma will keep to himself, how much the other fella will get his hands on.''

Lafe nodded thoughtfully. ''Stir up the pot, see what comes to the top, huh?''

''Something like that.''

''Well, I've got to admit, that's pretty much the way I been figurin'. Another reason why I kept you out here. To tell you the truth, I don't abide doing any more legwork than I have to. I think the two of us might be able to get somewhere on this.''

Cajun thought so too. He liked what he had seen of Lafe so far. He'd always known Lafe was a man who could handle himself and he could now see that Lafe was a man of some sense as well. On a whim, Cajun briefly considered letting him in on his plans for the silver, then just as quickly decided against it. He might have to depend on Lafe sometime. No point in spoiling a possible friendship by bringing up the subject of money. Money makes you keep looking over your shoulder.

"What's your idea for a start?" said Lafe.

"Well, our best chance is with someone who scares easy and at the same time is just as greedy as the rest. He's got to be someone who's easily impressed."

Lafe smiled thinly as he mounted his roan. "Yeah. He's my choice too."

With Tobey in Gallino Station were Ave Laughlin and Levi Ruffner. Levi and Tobey played blackjack while Ave sat by and helped with the bottle, keeping an eye on the windows for anyone coming to settle accounts for the day before. The only new company rode in across the flat to the north early in the afternoon. It was Miles Forber, a partner in the store in Sloan. Draped behind the cantle of his saddle were twin gunnysacks tied together, both of them bulging. Forber hoisted them over his shoulder after dismounting and waddled inside. The Sloan boys looked up eagerly when they heard the clink of bottles coming from inside the sacks.

Ave called out to the back room. "Get your ass out here, Joe! Miles' here to keep us in juice for the month."

"The week, more like," Levi said, wearing a lopsided grin.

Anson ambled from the back to the bar as the thick-set merchant put his goods on the counter.

"Got something for you," Forber said in his hearty, doing-business voice. "Just came in from the south. Fifteen bottles of mescal."

The sacks were opened and a couple of bottles taken out. Anson turned them around in his hand, judging them by sight. Forber gave him a price and

Anson disagreed and they haggled for awhile until the station owner was allowed to sample the merchandise. A round was set up for everyone. When Tobey and Levi returned to their game with their shots, Forber turned their way and said, "Haven't seen you boys in town the past few days. Ain't you afraid you're missing something?"

Levi flashed a knowing glance at Tobey. "Oh, we been keepin' busy. No worry about that."

The pop-eyes in Forber's swollen face took on a glint. "Well, I'll say you should have been there today. You know those two Mex whores, Anna and Margarita?"

Through a ripple of laughter, the boys said that they did.

"Well, that one, Margarita, she come into town today. She'd come down from Red Rock with some rancher yesterday and was on her way back when she came by. I asked her if she was doing any business today and you know what she said? She says she just thought she might run into that cute little kid she liked so much last time. She said, 'Where's that Tobay?' You know the way she talks. 'Where's that leetle Tobay?' she says."

"She did not!" Tobey said through his snorting laughter.

"She did so. Why would I lie?"

Levi laughed and shoved Tobey's shoulder.

"And she said," Forber added, "that she was staying the rest of the afternoon. She said if I saw you I should let you know."

"She did not!"

"Tobey, it's the God's honest truth. I got no reason to lead you on. Hell, I tried to get my piece but it was no doing. I ain't gettin' any happier telling you about it."

Ave shouted from the bar, "Hey Tobey, time for you to get in the saddle, huh?"

Tobey's pinched face reddened. He scratched his scalp as the laughter surrounded him.

Levi said that Margarita always liked them young and Ave needled that maybe Tobey wasn't up to it. Tobey denied she'd said it once again; then, after taking another punch in the shoulder, muttered, "Hell," long and low and got up for the door, detouring just long enough for another shot of mescal. The men were still hooting when the kid was saddled and headed across the flat.

Turning back to the bar, Miles Forber quickly ran a finger along the inside of his stiff collar and flicked it away from his wet neck. It was a hot day, but not that hot. Forber, unlike his partner Schliessen, was frankly frightened of these men. He was relieved that his favor to Jenkins was now completed.

Tobey was well into the high ground when he brought his horse over to the downside of a hogback and heard the voice call his name from behind. He reined suddenly and jerked his animal around.

To his rear, just come out of a draw, was Cajun Lee sitting on his black.

"Glad I found you, Tobey. There's something I want to talk to you about."

Tobey saw that Cajun's hands—both empty—were resting on the pommel. The kid tugged his reins, forced his horse around, and dug in for a sprint.

"Stop it there, Tobey, or I drop you."

The voice came from the side. Sweat streaming down his face, Tobey strained to see its source. Lafe strode out from behind the butte to the right, a dark scowl on his face and the Winchester in his hands. Lafe cocked the rifle with a sudden snap motion.

"Just one move," he growled, "and I'll blow you apart."

Cajun walked the black up to Tobey's side. With an even voice he said, "You ride right to the front of me, Tobey, and Lafe'll take the lead. Like I said, we want to talk."

They took him to the east about two miles and told him to dismount outside an abandoned shack amidst a patch of piñon. Inside was a table and chairs, a rug for a bed, and a strip of space to walk around in. Lafe pushed Tobey into one of the chairs.

"All right, kid, where'd you hid the cattle?"

Lafe was behind the chair. Tobey had to crane his neck to look at him. "What you mean? The Mex cattle?"

Lafe yanked the chair around to face him. "No, I don't mean the Mex cattle! I mean the Tolfane stock!"

Stepping closer, Cajun told the range detective to ease up.

"I will not ease up. Clell was a friend of mine and these bastards killed him. Now, kid—talk."

Tobey bit his sun-cracked lips and wiped the sweat out of his eye. "Shit, I don't know. I wasn't with that bunch. I went to the Mex ranches with Billy."

"You know where they are, you son of a bitch, so start talking."

"Hold on, Lafe." Cajun had a hand on the range detective's arm. "He'll start talking. You just got him crazy scared. He can't think straight with you acting like this, right Tobey?"

"Y-Yeah. Yeah, that's right. I can't think straight."

Lafe glowered at the outlaw, then yanked his arm free from Cajun's grip, moving away a couple of steps. Cajun turned a smile towards Tobey and, reaching inside his serape, pulled out a bottle of whiskey from inside his waistband.

"Now we're going to have us a drink and relax and think about it. We got the whole day."

He uncorked the bottle, took a swig and passed it over to Lafe. The range detective took his swallow, his eyes still glued to Tobey, and stepped back towards him. He took another swallow. His mouth worked in agitation.

"You want a drink, Tobey?" he asked.

The kid nodded apprehensively.

Lafe studied him a moment more. His right eye then narrowed and his lip curled as he cried, "You want a drink!" He smashed the bottle across the side of the table and whipped the jagged bottle handle over to Tobey's face. "You son of a bitch, you're not getting nothing from me, you bastard, you're going to talk and then we'll see if we let you live, you—"

Cajun jumped him from behind, pinned his arms back and swung him around fast, running him flat into the wall. Lafe cursed and tried thrashing his arms to loosen the grip, but Cajun grabbed Lafe's right wrist and slammed it against the wall, making him drop the bottle handle. Lafe bucked the hold. Cajun caught the man's neck between his arms and

99

pinned him to the side. Tobey watched wide-eyed as, a few moments later, Lafe's body relaxed and the man in the serape slowly loosed his hold.

"That's it, Lafe," he said. "Now we're going to get some talking done. You hear?"

Lafe grunted yes.

"You're going outside and then me and Tobey are going to talk things over. You know I'm doing the right thing."

The chief range detective straightened and nodded, his breath working hard. Cajun had him out the door in another minute and turned back to Tobey, slowing himself with a long breath. He took a seat at the table.

"I remember you, Tobey, from that night in the cantina with the Claibournes. You were going along with them, but you didn't throw down on me and that figures in with me. I know you're not like the rest."

"That's right, mister," Tobey said rapidly. "That was their idea, I didn't want no part of that. That was them, not me, mister."

"The name's Cajun. It's time we got acquainted. Now you take your time and you tell me what you know about the whereabouts of the stock. You got nothing to be afraid of with me."

Tobey took a little while to settle his nerves, then started his story. He said he had been riding with the Mexican herd and had no way of knowing where the Tolfane cattle was taken. He didn't even know where his bunch ended up. After setting up the barricade in the draw, Billy Laughlin had sent him back to find out if and when the detectives and the Mexicans had given up.

Cajun said, "And no one told you where they

were hid?''

"Uh-uh. I asked but they didn't tell. They said it was just as well I didn't know." Under his breath, he added, "I guess they didn't think they could trust me."

Cajun could believe that and didn't think the kid would know much more. Getting tough wouldn't help. He got up and walked to the window, looking out at Lafe. "You know how many head was in that Mex herd?"

"Yeah. About seventy-five, a hundred."

Cajun made a grunting noise of acknowledgement as he mulled this over for awhile. "I don't know off-hand how many was in the Tolfane stock, but I guess it's more than that. All together that's going to come to quite a price." He faced the kid. "How much you getting for all your trouble, Tobey?"

"Well, I guess I don't know. It depends."

"Depends on what?"

"On what Johnny decides to give me. I'll get something, I just don't know what yet."

"That the way it is with the others, with the Claibournes and the Laughlins?"

"No. They each get a big piece and they split it up amongst themselves."

Cajun came closer, propping his feet up on his chair and leaning forward on his thigh. "Doesn't sound to me like you're getting much of a fair shake, Tobey." The kid looked down and didn't answer. "But I guess the Claibournes got to be treated special, don't they? I hear that's where Johnny lives, on the Claibourne place. Is that right?"

"Yeah. He's got the Old Man's room."

"Well, I can see why Johnny takes such good care of him. He's like part of the family. But you, just because you're not a Claibourne, you get thrown the scraps. That's a real shame."

Tobey looked up at him, his long face creasing on one side in confusion. He wanted to gripe, inspired by this man's sympathy, but another part of him was naturally uneasy and untrusting. Cajun, remembering what Joe Anson had told him, said, "The Claibourne ranch is west of Sloan, right? Somewhere northwest of Gallino Station?"

Tobey answered reluctantly, saying that it was.

"That's probably where Johnny stashes the loot that he doesn't give out to fellas like you. Now, I can tell, you think I'm trying to sell you something. That's just because you're smart enough to know better. But you know just as well as I do that what I'm saying is right. You deserve something better and those Claibournes are corn-holing you. They probably got things hid away around there you don't even know about and they got it in places they won't let you know about, just like they didn't let you in on where they left the cattle. Am I right?"

Tobey felt one part of him coming irresistably to the surface. "That's right. Yes sir, I bet they do."

Cajun was quick to follow it up. "And they probably make the decisions for the rest of you, not letting you even come to the ranch because you might see how much they got there all to themselves."

"Now, that's not true. I can go to the Claibourne. I been there lots of times. And whenever there's something to decide, they ask me there."

Unbelieving, Cajun said, "They let you make

102

the plans with them? I can't see that because I know you're smart enough that if you were making the plans, you would make sure you got a bigger share."

"Well, it's true that's it's not exactly like that. Mainly it's Johnny what decides. He kind of leaves for awhile and makes up his mind and then comes back. But I been there. I can go there any time."

Cajun edged closer. "Johnny leaves for awhile? Where does he go?"

Tobey dropped his gaze to the floor again, but it wasn't just a natural reluctance to talk this time. Tobey had a hand gripping the edge of the table and the knuckles were turning white. Cajun asked once more where Johnny would go.

"Someplace. He just goes someplace to think."

Cajun couldn't catch Tobey's eye. He took this as an answer in itself. Moving without hurry, he took hold of his serape and shifted it to the side, showing the black Colt in its holster. Tobey's eyes flicked up. Cajun spoke in a hard-edged monotone.

"I got something to confess to you, Tobey. When we came in here, Lafe was getting rough and you were scared shitless, but then when I put him out you calmed down because you knew I was being reasonable. Well, that was all an act. You think Lafe is wild? It's not that way. I'm the one he steps aside for. And another thing I lied about. I told you I thought you were smart. That's not true. I'm asking you a question and you're not answering and that's dumber than hell."

Tobey's slit eyes were fixed on the holstered gun. Cajun could see him try to suppress a swallow.

"Now you talk, kid. Where does Baehma go off

to?"

Tobey rubbed a hand across his mouth. "Shit, I don't know, I swear it. Nobody knows that."

"Come on, try harder."

"I can't tell you nothin' more." He shifted about in his seat. "It's the Old Man's place is all I know. It's up in the hills somewhere. I ain't been there. That's where the Old Man buried his last wife and that's where he used to go to think up our new deals. Not even Claibournes are allowed."

"How come Johnny is?"

"When he was taking over, the Old Man took him up there, made him like family even though he wasn't."

"Didn't nobody ever follow Baehma up there?"

The thin voice exploded. "No! You can't do that. No tellin' what Johnny'd do if he found someone doin' that. Morgan told me he followed him up there once but I don't believe him. Nobody does that."

"Morgan, huh?"

"He musta been lyin'. Nobody'd try that."

Cajun squinted, as if peering through a haze, imagining the power of these family ties that could even spook someone who wasn't a relation. Tobey sat hunched over, his right hand digging into his left arm, his face glazed with fear. He had told all he knew.

Cajun brought his foot down from the chair and paced away. "You're a bunch of damn fools," he said, the words grating in his throat. "And you in particular. Baehma could have thousands up there, maybe more, and you just go on doing everything he tells you." He leveled a piercing, contemptuous glare at the outlaw, half felt, half for effect. He made an abrupt motion toward the door. "Go on, get the hell out of here. You make me sick."

Tobey took only a moment to absorb his sudden turn of luck, then stepped lightly from the chair, hurrying into a scramble once he reached the door. Cajun came out to watch him climb into the saddle and canter off, not bothering to ask for the return of his revolver.

Coming to the hogback where he had been taken in, Tobey slowed his horse to a walk and tried clearing his mind to consider which way he would go. He quickly decided against going to Sloan, electing instead to go to the Ruffner place and hole up by himself with a bottle for awhile before showing his face anywhere.

Heading south, he crossed a basin and was shortly prodding his animal through a switchback lined with cottonwood. Beyond a turn by a clump of boulders, he paused for a swig from his canteen.

"Keep your hands where they are, Tobey."

The voice came from his rear. He froze in place.

"Don't worry, Tobey. I just want to talk over that little meeting you just had."

11

The tracking of Spider Pass was painstaking, tedious work made worse by the hardpan land that cooked up to a blasting heat. For all their efforts, the range detectives got only minimal results that insured their return the next day for more of the same. They had ruled out the pass on the right, though, which gave Lafe more leeway with the deployment of the men. He left his two best trackers, Caldwell and Charley Benton, to work the left route with Heck Buel as the cover on top. Ray Pence and Phin he sent out to the surrounding ranches. He then rode off with Cajun Lee, circling around the high ground and heading to the east

Coming out of a cutbank arroyo onto the sage flat west of Gallino Station, Lafe and Cajun mapped out their work for the day.

"We're best off," Cajun said, "starting with the outsiders in the group. Those in the family are tied in too close. At least it seemed that way from talking to Tobey. He'd be a good way in himself but the others are just smart enought to know not to tell him too much."

"He still might be worth something. If he gets more greedy he'll talk about it and maybe get someone else to thinking."

"Could be. But no one's going to pay him much

mind if he's on his own."

"Which leaves Ruffner and Morgan Fleet for today. I'll take Fleet. He and Josh Claibourne went to Gallino Station last night. When they leave today, Claibourne'll likely go his own way to his ranch which would leave Fleet along."

Cajun said he supposed so in a mechanical way, while he tried to think of an idea to work things around. "Guess I could find Ruffner at his ranch, scout it out, see if I can get in without trouble. But if it's all the same to you, I'd rather go with Fleet."

"I think not. I've gotten to know Fleet pretty good and he can be a curly one. It's not like putting something over on Tobey. I'd best take him."

"You may be right, Lafe," Cajun said, pausing to stare meaningfully down towards his pommel, "but it'd mean something special to me if I went for him."

Lafe cocked his head slightly to the side as he regarded the man in the serape. "What would that mean?"

"Well, Morgan Fleet, he's the one who killed Clell Forrest. Now Clell didn't mean that much to me, but it's the way these Sloan boys work. I can't abide it. I want Fleet."

Lafe took his time before answering. "You plannin' on doing something other than talking?"

"I'm not counting on it. Our plan's the same as far as I'm concerned. I just want to take my turn with him. To size him up, I guess."

Studying him for another moment, Lafe shook his head. "You're a surprising feller, Cajun. I wouldn't have thought it would make that much difference to you." He raked the landscape as he rode on, then slowly turned back to Cajun, the slightest hint of a smile playing across his scored face. "I'll be going to Ruffner's."

"Obliged."

The inscrutable face gave Cajun little idea of whether the range detective was seeing through his manipulation. It didn't seem to matter, for he was surprised to find that the very fact that he was trying to deceive the range detective was getting under his own skin. Once more he thought that maybe he should play it straight with this man. Once again he decided that that would be unwise. The thin line Cajun was straddling meant taking added risk. Lafe was a square dealer doing his job and he shouldn't be exposed to more trouble than he already had.

Turning east at Dragoon Pass, Cajun set out on his own toward Gallino Station. During his last ride in this direction he had noticed a bluff a few miles from the station that would serve as a good lookout. On its blind side was a trail leading down and around to the flat that could be traveled fast when he'd seen what he was looking for. A few miles through these hills and he would reach the trail, leaving him some time to spare before the two Sloan men would be making their morning ride out.

At first he didn't lay much credence to it, only aware of it on the outermost reaches of his senses—seeming to be more like an unconscious, instinctive turn of mind than something actually heard. But this was just the sort of thing that necessity had taught him to rely on. He rode on, working to sort out all sounds except those from his rear. He continued like this for fifteen, twenty minutes before he heard it again—a faint, raspy sound. Further on up the gradual grade while following a bend in the trail he saw two jackrabbits in a small clearing some fifty yards below scampering across the pass, scared by something. Near the top of the grade he finally caught a passing glimpse of the rider going behind a shoulder. Whoever it was, he wasn't afraid to get too close.

Cajun topped the path, rode on twenty yards, doubled back about half that distance along a strip of rock to the side of the trail, swung behind a close-set pair of boulders, and dismounted for the wait.

It was only one man—which made it unlikely that it was one of Baehma's gang. They seemed to be fond of company, although the possibility of a lone rider could not be ruled out. The thought occurred to Cajun that Lafe could be more suspicious than he had expected. He then cleared his mind, pulling his Colt and concentrating on the rider's approach.

The clop of hoofs was not long in coming. Cajun moved silently to the downhill side of the boulder and flattened his back against its side, his gun pointed skyward, poised for sudden movement. The walking hoofbeats reached the near side of the twin boulders and soon drew alongside. The rider cleared and the Colt snapped forward, hammer snapping back.

The horseman reined, made no other movement, stared straight ahead. At the sight of him Cajun frowned with tired realization.

He said, "Come up on me one more time, Phin, and I'll kill you."

Phin turned slowly to face him, the curled tightening lip into a straight thin line. He tried for a bluff tone. "Fellow employees shouldn't hold each other under the gun now, should they, Cajun?"

"Cut the shit and start talking. What were you back-trailing for?"

"I wasn't tailing you."

Cajun grimaced with impatience. "You sure as hell looked like it, so get talking. I'm not going to dance around with you."

"You're right, I was tailing you—but not at first. It just happens we're after the same thing."

Cajun let the gun rest back in his palm and paced towards Phin's front, regarding the round-shouldered man intently. "Can't say as I'm really surprised. I knew you had something sticking up your rear. You were the one who talked to Joe Anson before I got to him."

Phin said that he was.

"You found out about Fleet going up to the Old Man's place, or at least saying that he did. You get that from Tobey also?"

"That too. I got him after you and Lafe were through with him. You did a good job. He was talking almost before I finished my questions."

"Glad you appreciate it." He holstered the gun and eased down on the rock behind him. Running his thumb along his moustache, he said, "Seems like we got something to talk over."

Phin swung down off the horse. "Seems like we do."

"Now I suppose one of us could bushwack the other the first chance he gets. But that'd leave all sorts of questions to be answered with Tolfane and the others and that'd probably mean more problems that it's worth. You with me so far?"

"I guess you're right."

Pushing his flat-brimmed hat back, he continued. "Well, we're both after the silver and since it doesn't look like Baehma's been spending it yet there should still be a lot of it. Actually there's really not that much talking to do after all. As much as it pains me, it looks like we're going to have to throw in together on this."

"Don't get so suffered about it, Cajun. I ain't so pleased about taking just half myself."

"Yeah. I thought I'd see some of that tough talk as soon as I'd put the gun away."

Phin's deep set eyes flicked angrily at him, but no words followed.

"I guess," Cajun said, "we can look at it this way. This could cut our work in half and being greedy could just trip a man up."

"There's something else too. What about Lafe? He's in it too, isn't he?"

"No, he isn't."

"You two were talking to Tobey. You saying he didn't know what was going on?"

"I'm saying he's not in it because I worked it out that way."

The skin on the outside of Phin's eyes creased. "You expect me to believe that? How'm I to know you two won't be crowdin' me out?"

"I tell you, I would be an idiot if I expected anything from you." He stood up to meet Phin eye to eye. "And another thing, you try anything with me or you just try telling me what we should do and I'm going to leave you out in the cold, one way or the other. You understand me?"

Phin held his gaze uncertainly for a moment, then averted his eyes briefly, bringing them back up to assert himself the best he could. "All right then, we're partners."

Cajun turned on his heels, mounted in one long
sudden step and reined the horse around toward
the downslope trail. He had half expected to find
some competition along the way so he told himself
he had no reason to be this bitter with the company
he had found. After all, these were the rules he had
set up for himself. Glancing cooly at Phin who was
saddling up, Cajun judged he had at least found
someone he was willing to share the risk with.

"Let's find Fleet," he said, and cantered down
the slope.

12

Along the rim of the basin, Fleet was pulled off his horse and stiff-armed until he was backed up against the steep rise that climbed to the plain above. Morgan Fleet watched sullenly as the other one, the one in the serape, dismounted and joined his friend. Still neither one spoke. They hadn't said a word since sneaking up on him along the bluff near Gallino Station. The silence was beginning to wear on Fleet. His high forehead was beaded with sweat that was only partly due to the heat. If he was killed out here there would be no one to know.

Cajun said, "You're looking nervous, Morgan. I heard you had more nerve than that."

"What the hell you want?" He spat out the words to keep up the front.

"Slow down. You're talking to reasonable men. That means we won't hurt you unless you give us a reason. There's something we want you to help us out on."

"Like what? The cattle?"

"That's part of it. You feel like telling us something about that?"

Fleet had a dark complexioned, square-jawed face with high cheek bones that suggested Indian blood. The face now bristled with defiance as he answered, "There won't be nothing I'll be telling you. You can try forcing me but you don't know how close to the stock you are. The others hear anything, they'll be coming down here to take care of you fast.''

"That right?" Phin said. "Maybe we should just take you back to the ranch and see what we can do there. We'll have lots of time and there ain't no one there to object to what happens to you.''

"Not after what happened to Clell," Cajun put in. Fleet faced him unflinchingly, only a slight twitch at a corner of the mouth contradicting his seeming confidence. "Of course, maybe you want to talk about other things first." Fleet wouldn't give in with a reply. "For one thing, I heard you've been up to the Old Man's place, where he buried his wife.''

"Can't account for what you hear.''

Phin grabbed the outlaw's shirtfront. "We're not asking you to account for anything. We just—''

Cajun put an arm across the other range detective. "We're just telling you what we know, fella. And we know you been saying that you followed Johnny up to the Old Man's place and that's what we're talking about here.''

Phin released his grip and backed off a step. Fleet shot a questioning glance at the two men before him. Cajun went on.

"Now I don't know if you really did or not. But one thing I do know is that at least you got the nerve to lie about something like this. And I know that makes you different from the others. The Claibournes and Laughlins would sweat bullets just thinking about saying that.''

Cajun let this sit with the outlaw for a couple of

114

moments. Fleet rubbed his unshaven throat and glowered at the man in the serape.

"What you after?" he finally asked.

Phin punctuated his words with a finger poking the air. "What we want is Baehma, plain and simple. We get rid of him, we get rid of our trouble. If you're smart, you'll help us."

"And you'll be standing up for yourself," Cajun said. "Baehma's looking out for himself, it's about time you did the same. It's no secret what he uses the place in the hills for. And whatever he stashes up there could be just as much yours. If you want to do right by yourself, then maybe we can make us some kind of deal."

Fleet's gaze drifted into the distance, his mouth twisting to one side.

"Like Phin said, we can also just take you back to Tolfane's place. But that won't be worth as much to either of us." Plainly the implication didn't have to be spelled out as much with this man as with Tobey. Cajun's piece was said and it was still vague enough for more than one thing to be made of it. His next move would have to depend on Fleet's response. The outlaw was about to speak when Cajun picked up a sound to the side, to the right. He pivoted, quickly identified it as a muffled hoof, and then just as quickly came to the queasy realization that it was too close. The other two turned in time to see four riders topping the saddle forty or fifty feet away. It was Robles, Urbina, Camilo Lucero and Tomas. They reined in for a moment, then, seeing no move was being made, started down the bare slope.

"Give me my gun back," Fleet hissed. "We can take 'em."

Cajun half-turned to him. "Keep the hell quiet."

Phin darted his partner an unsure glance but didn't say anything or move his hands.

The four Mexicans drew up one alongside the other. Robles pointed to Morgan Fleet. "Where are you taking him?"

Cajun said, "Now that's up to us, isn't it?"

Robles brought himself up straight, his dark eyes smouldering. "He is one of those who had my sister. He goes with us."

The Mexicans were all armed with revolvers in their belts and rifles in their saddle sheaths. As yet none of them had pulled anything out into the open. Cajun spoke slowly and evenly but with an edge to his voice. "We're out here looking for our cattle. That's what you got to do also. We found this man here so we could learn something and if you four knew what you were doing you'd be out doing the same. You're getting off the track here, friend, and you should know it."

Robles's expression drew tight. "We did not come down here to ask for your advice, mister. This man has to pay for something and we will take him whether you want to give him up or not."

"All I can say is you'd be better off if you didn't try."

Morgan Fleet eyed Phin's horse. Sticking out of the saddle bag was the handle of his Colt but the animal was at least ten feet away. He'd be dead before he could reach it. And he was on the wrong side of Phin to grab for the range detective's gun, which ruled out the second possibility.

Robles glanced at the three men beside him and turned back to Cajun. "There are four of us here and only two of you with guns. That's not much of a chance."

"It is for the only one who's got his gun cleared."

All eyes turned to Cajun. On his left side, his hand was visible just below the edge of his black serape. His right hand was hidden somewhere, but a slight bulge showed where his right arm was crooked. Phin turned to the Mexicans with a grin creasing his face, his own gun hand poised.

Cajun stared directly at Robles. "You been doing the talking so I figure you're the one giving orders. Now I don't know how many of you I can get but one thing's for sure. You're going to be a dead man on the first shot." He swept the other three quickly to see that they were still. "Which is it going to be, jefe?"

Lucero, Urbina, and Tomas sent uncertain looks toward their leader. Enraged, Robles stared at the man in the serape with eyes dark as coal, his knuckles whitening as he gripped the reins. For several moments he stayed like that. Lucero tentatively backed his horse a couple of steps; Urbina and Tomas reined their animals into quarter turns. In a minute Robels swung around and led the way back to the slope, his shoulders stooped.

Cajun holstered the Colt once they had ridden out of view on the other side. "Let's move. They could change their minds." He went over to his black, then gathered the reins for Fleet's horse, leading it over to the outlaw.

While handing over the reins, he detected a wary appreciation in the way Fleet looked at him. He could see that the Mexicans may have done more for him than he could have expected to do on his own.

"We're letting you go," he said. "You better make good time of it." He then told Phin to turn over the gun.

Fleet glanced at Cajun with narrowed eyes and got into the saddle without answering. Cajun grabbed the pommel before he could start off.

"Just keep in mind what the Mexicans plan to do with you. And think about what kind of deal you're getting with Baehma. Ask yourself who you're best working with."

Morgan Fleet prodded the horse away. "I'll think about it." He rode off at a fast trot. As the two range detectives saddled up, Phin asked Cajun if he thought the outlaw would come through.

"I don't know that he'll just walk on over to us, but he'll do something. We'll have to play it as it goes."

The Mexicans rode away from the basin at a deliberate walk, the silence hanging heavy. Robles stopped, turned slowly around, and stared thoughtfully at their back-trail. Wheeling around, Urbina pulled up alongside him.

"We go back, Diego? They would be ready for us, if they are still there at all."

Robles' absent expression didn't change. "No, we won't go back."

Urbina watched curiously as Robles sat upon his horse. For a few hopeful moments, the jefe imagined what he could do with a couple of men like Cajun Lee on his side.

13

The night air about Gallino Station was cool and still. For the moment, the air was the same inside.

Josh Claibourne swiveled in his chair to face the bar and break the silence. "Morg," he called, "what you say you try yourself a hand or two?"

Fleet took his eyes from his half-filled glass. "Not tonight," he said in a restrained voice. Coming from his seat at the game table, Tobey joined Fleet at the counter. Without looking at Josh, he put in, "I gotta be a fool to try beatin' you Claibournes at blackjack. You take all my damn money away."

"You just threw me a few hands. You give up too soon, is all."

Tobey took the bottle to refill his glass and the quiet resumed. Josh checked to see Ave Laughlin still asleep at the table across the way. Annoyed, he scanned the three men in the room with him. "Ave, get the hell up! Ave!"

Laughlin stirred, raised his head from the table with a start, shook himself, and focused his nearly closed eyes on Josh.

"Get over here, Ave. These other fellers are afraid to put their money down. I guess it takes family to get up a game."

Ave groaned a lazy negative answer, reaching for

the bottle in front of him. Claibourne shook his head.

"You are some crowd, ain't ya. First day I feel back to myself and I come in here to wind up with a bunch of old ladies. Shit, you'd think you were the ones got shot up."

"Lay off us, Josh." It was Morgan Fleet.

"What the hell's your problem, Morg? We got a whole passel of new steer and there's that cache of silver and you stand around with a long face. We got us a good run here. You'd think a feller'd want to act like it."

"Maybe we would if we had the money to do it with."

"You can't expect it just like that. Cattle don't mean money till you sell 'em."

Fleet turned back around to the bar, muttering, "You Claibournes always seem to have it." He pivoted when he heard the chair scraping back against the wooden floor. Josh was on his feet, striding towards him.

"What the hell is eatin' you, Morg?"

"Don't you come at me like that, Josh—I'm warnin' you!"

"Maybe you want to take it outside if you're so burnin' up!"

Ave was awake enough to get himself moving in a hurry. He grabbed Josh's arm and shoved him back against the bar as Tobey stepped in front of Fleet, telling him to cool down. Josh shouted as he struggled against his cousin's hold.

"I want to know what the hell you mean by that! What the hell you tryin' to say?"

Fleet made no move to get past Tobey and after a few busy, noisy moments Ave had Josh out of the fighting mood. The two men exchanged a glaring look.

Remembering what he had in mind to do, Fleet then held himself in check and let caution gain control. He downed the rest of his drink and when he spoke his tone was surprisingly even.

"I didn't mean nothin' by that, Josh. I was just talkin'."

"Didn't sound like just talk to me."

"I must be gettin' a little edgy about having to tend stock tonight. Guess I just talked too much."

"You see that," said Ave. "Wasn't nothin' to it, Josh. Just ease down and let it slide."

Claibourne mulled it over irritably and decided to take this advice. To seal the peace, Anson lined up the glasses and they all went another round. When it was finished, Fleet picked up his saddle bag and said he'd be on his way.

"What's your hurry?" Ave said, pulling out the stolen gold watch from his vest pocket. "It's not even eleven-thirty. Johnny said he'd be by around midnight to tell us when to take the next shift."

"I'll be there around twelve, don't worry. I just don't feel like sittin'. Think I'll give my horse some exercise." On his way out the door, he thought of what he really wanted to say. Be damned if I need Johnny to tell me when to go.

Around ten to twelve Baehma and Levi Ruffner tied their horses to the front rail and walked in. They found Ave obliging his cousin with a few hands and Tobey still standing at the bar, his eyes red-rimmed and his posture more slouched than usual. After finding out where Fleet had gone, Baehma moved to the bar and got a closer look at Tobey. He took the bottle from the kid's hand.

121

"You had enough about an hour ago by the look of you. What do you think you're doing? You got to keep alert till dawn."

"I know how much I can take." He grabbed for the bottle. Baehma yanked it out of his reach, taking hold of Tobey's shirtfront with the other hand.

"You heard me, you runt!"

"Leave him be, Johnny."

Baehma spun his head to see Levi Ruffner standing a few paces away. His hands were curled around the front of his gun belt, a stance that could be either casual or threatening. The outlaw chief faced Tobey and saw the cast of the kid's face suddenly change. With the backing-up from Ruffner, the usual timid subservience gave way to defiance. Tentativeness lay behind it, but for the first time since Baehma had known him there was enough grit in the kid to show through.

"No call for you to do that," the kid blurted, his lower lip quivering.

Now for the first time since Tobey had known the man, there was a strange look to Johnny Baehma—one of confusion. Back-talk like this was unthinkable. Ordinarily Tobey would have found himself on the floor, in a condition that would have made it hard to get up again. Baehma's green eyes wavered. He then collected himself. He heaved Tobey aside like a doll and bellied up to the bar. In a low growl he said, "Nobody stands to my back."

Ruffner's hatchet face slacked. He turned and walked silently to the near table with retiring stride.

His position regained, Baehma tried untangling what had just happened. He knew that for a brief moment he had shown weakness. Two of his men had stood up to him and he had almost lost the nerve to recover his ground. He had allowed himself to be unprepared for something and the surprise had hobbled him. Even now he was trying to account for what had happened. Everything was going their way, all the money was coming in. What was there to gripe about, damn it? He stopped on that thought, his mind clearing away the temporary quandary. Everyone knew about men falling out over money as soon as there was more than enough around. The only problem was that the outlaw chief had become too confident about his hold over the men. That would change right away! He turned to face the others.

To one side, Josh and Ave continued their game quietly. Their sporadic monosyllables and the slap of the cards provided a rhythmic backdrop of sound in an otherwise noiseless room. Tobey sat brooding in one corner and Ruffner was at a table on the other side, idly running his hat through his hands.

Baehma said, "We spotted the greasers tryin' to trail us to one of the hideaways today. We were able to lose 'em but we got to watch ourselves until we have the chance to put 'em away. We need some more good horses so I'll be goin' to buy some over at Blackmun's tomorrow."

A grunt of acknowledgement from Ave was all the reply he got. Damn them all, Baehma thought. It's not their conversation I need. He told them all to get off their cans and take their shifts if it was their turn and to move fast. Although he had finished his work for the night, Ruffner left with the others. Baehma waited till they were receding in the distance and, after taking a shot of mescal, went outside to mount the steeldust. He rode to the southwest, heading for the Old Man's place in the hills.

Some time later, he prodded the quarter horse up and around the last shoulder and came down the lip at a walk. The light from the moon and the stars filled the small hollow with a pale, brownish glow broken by the shadowed ruts. In the center was the mound with the jagged slab serving as its headstone. To the side, set into the sheer wall, was the cave. Baehma tethered his horse, went into the cave, felt around in the dark for just enough silver to buy the horses, and came back out.

He stood by the grave of the Old Man's wife, gazing off into the distance. From this spot a man could see for miles across the desert to the south, the view obstructed only off to the left where a sharply cut skyline loomed darkly about halfway to the horizon. The Old Man had picked his place well. Many times, as now, Baehma could stand here and feel everything pull away from him except what lay before his eyes. After that, his mind would be ready to figure through any predicament.

He left the side of the grave thinking that the squabble that night could never lead to anything out of hand. He boarded the steeldust, climbed out of the hollow, and wove his way downward, not hearing the intruder till he was a couple of miles towards the level.

He heard the rustle of a branch somewhere across the face of the slope. He considered circling around to sneak up on whoever it was, but in the darkness he thought a maneuver like that might backfire. Continuing down instead, he switched over trails every chance he had, and by the time he reached the north end of the hills he was sure he had lost his man. The thought then hit him that maybe the back-trailer had no interest in following him way back to the ranch to set up an ambush. The back-trailer may have been careless enough to reveal himself because he had already found out what he had come for. Baehma's stomach wrenched and his mind cluttered with wild suspicion.

From a rise well above, Morgan Fleet watched Baehma cross the flat at a trot. Cajun Lee was right. Until now, Fleet had only had the nerve to lie about following Baehma into the hills. But now he knew.

He saddled up and left for the early morning shift at the cattle hideaway. He could still make it before Ave and Josh would have doubts about his leaving early.

14

The second day of tracking narrowed the field to a single quadrant to the southeast of Spider Pass. The area covered several square miles, all of it covered with the usual torturous trails, only one of which led to the hideout. Buel, Caldwell, and Benton worked into the night for the final effort, assisted at nightfall by Ray Pence; but it was too black then and the men were too fatigued to do much good. They returned to the Tolfane ranch for some sleep and at first light the next morning the range detectives came out in full force to comb the area.

Lafe divided the men into two groups. Caldwell, Benton, Buel and Pence covered the western half, while Cajun Lee and Phin worked the other with Lafe—the eastern section rating a man less because the land was somewhat flatter and more open.

Once when Lafe was out of hearing, Phin moved close to Cajun and said that one of them should make an excuse to range off and do something about the silver. Cajun told him that finding the cattle would work to their benefit by making the Sloan bunch more desperate and more likely to fight amongst themselves. When this explanation left Phin unconvinced, Cajun reminded him who was making the decisions and—apart from a little grumbling, Phin showed no inclination to test him.

By midday, Lafe, Cajun, and Phin were following up a possibility through a draw winding east across a level. They stopped at noon beneath a cluster of willows.

Jesse Laughlin sidled up to the crest of the hogback and, peering over, could see the three men amidst the clump of trees below, some fifty yards off. He stayed put till he was sure he recognized them, then backed down the pitch, led his horse away at a quiet walk, mounted up once out of earshot, and rode the last mile to the valley teeming with livestock.

Sol Claibourne had come by to help with changing the brands. Working with him at the north end of the valley were Billy and Levi Ruffner while Amos was outriding at the entrance on the other side. Billy, squatting by the fire and heating an iron, looked up as his brother Jesse reined in next to him. Jesse wiped the streams of sweat away from his beefy face, an urgent glint in his squinting eyes.

"They're comin', Billy."

Billy straightened up slowly while the other two looked away from the steer pinned to the ground. "How close?"

"Just over a short piece. By Ransum Draw."

Sol and Ruffner let go the steer. Sol stepped toward the fire.

"We move 'em on now? My shoulder ain't bad, I can do my share."

Billy scanned the herd thoughtfully. "We could make it to the next valley fast enough."

Jesse said, "I got a good look at them, Billy.

127

There's just three. One of 'em is that Cajun feller.''

Billy faced his brother, his eyes shining darkly. "Is that right?"

"Also Lafe Jenkins and one of the others."

Running his hand along the soft stubble on his chin, Billy turned to Sol and Ruffner. Amos, noticing the men by the fire grouped for a talk, walked his horse in their direction. Billy kicked sand into the fire and watched it sputter and die before he spoke.

"We get rid of these three detectives, we might not have to move the herd at all. We could save us some cow punchin'."

"Wait a minute," Ruffner said. "We start shooting and the cattle could get spooked. Won't be no one here to settle 'em if we're all out after these three."

"We're downwind from them, Levi. Won't be no problem with that. Sol here can stay behind just to be sure. Besides," and Billy's lips peeled back in a crooked smile, "I'd like to see how good this Cajun is. So far it's all talk."

Jesse let out a short, hoarse laugh. "And that Tobey's always been a liar. Like to see this feller with the tables turned myself."

Talking to Lafe the day before had left Levi with some questions. He wasn't counting on changing sides just yet but he thought he could use some time to think it over. Then again, if Lafe and the other two were out of the way, there was no telling how much the Sloan could make off with. There wouldn't be any need for a deal.

Amos drew up along the snuffed fire. He raked the faces with a flashing glance. "You been meetin' on somethin'?''

Ruffner said, "We going to bag us a couple of sinners, Amos."

Claibourne's left eye twitched and his incomplete row of teeth gleamed dully in a determined grimace. "Which way?" he said.

Leaving Sol behind, Billy, Jesse, Amos, and Ruffner rode off for Ransum Draw. They reached the hogback to find the three detectives still under the trees, tightening the cinches on their saddles.

"Pick 'em off from here?" Jesse asked his brother.

"No good. The trees'll give 'em cover. We'll have to get close. Amos and Levi, you go down the draw on foot. When you get across from them for a crossfire, me and Jesse'll ride down at 'em. When they turn our way, you cut loose. Move fast, before they saddle up."

Taking their rifles and loading them up, Amos and Ruffner skirted along the base of the ridge and headed for the draw.

The detectives let their animals browse the grass a few moments more before taking up for the afternoon. Cajun took his last bite of jerky and was looking off to the south, wondering how long he could keep up his patience with Phin. He was an able enough man when he was occupied with the right thing, but his temper could flare at any time and Cajun couldn't be sure it was only the man's disposition at the core of it. But these thoughts disappeared when he saw the two figures appear above the hogback. He turned and was running for the rifle in his saddle boot before the horses cleared the crest.

Closer to his animal, Lafe yanked his Winchester, levered, and aimed. Gunfire cracked from the side and the three detectives flattened to the ground. Bullets hissed above them and whined off of trees. Cajun took his face out of the dirt to see the two Laughlins come down off the ridge and drum across the flat, handguns drawn. Lafe rolled behind a willow and Phin dove for the cover of another. Lafe answered the fire from the draw with his rifle, Phin with his revolver. In the short pause in shooting from the side, Cajun jumped to his feet, sprinted for his black, vaulted into the saddle a la Mexicana, and spurred out of the willow patch on the side away from the draw. One thing was clear in his mind. The Sloan men had them where they wanted them and there were no good odds in staying put.

Clear of the trees, he swung wide to his left and broke into a blistering gallop across the front-trail of the Laughlins, jerking the black Colt from its holster. He got off five shots in the space of a long breath, sending them in a fan-like pattern. Still thirty yards off, Jesse automatically reined sharply, his horse rearing into harsh stop. Billy veered to the side, to Cajun's rear, triggering fast. One slug cut a swathe across the black's haunches, Cajun beat a path for a smooth slope into the draw up ahead. He took the top of the grade at a gallop, then suddenly drew in to a canter and wheeled violently into the base of the draw amid a thick swirl of dust. He bent forward and tugged the black's head down to keep himself and the animal below the edge of cover. He coughed the dust out of his mouth and nose, waited for the air to clear so he could open his eyes to a squint, and ejected the spent shells

130

from the cylinder. Without replacing the cartridges, he holstered the gun and drew the Spencer.

He could place the gunmen up ahead at about forty, fifty feet away. Taking hold of both the reins and the barrel of the rifle in his left hand, he calculated the effect of an armed horseman bearing down on a man boxed in a cut and then kneed the black forward.

He lifted the animal to a gallop as he rounded a bend and came within sight of Amos Ruffner. He let out a yell and levered rapidly. The two men snapped their heads his way. Unaccustomed to the black's motion when firing at a run, Cajun wasn't able to hit his marks but his guess was right. The two outlaws squeezed a few hurried shots at the oncoming rider and then turned on their heels and backed off at a stumbling run. They fired back twice more to no effect before scrambling behind a shoulder for cover. Cajun immediately reined to the right—the side they had taken—where he was protected by the draw's curved wall.

He fired his last round, inserted a new cylinder, then took the time to load his Colt. The fire from the shoulder picked up. The shooting across the way toward the trees told him that Lafe and Phin were still at it. He finished loading, holstered the hand gun, and, lifting a knee to the seat of the saddle, brought the Spencer back up. He raised himself on the knee and fired over the draw's curved rim at Amos and Ruffner's position.

As Billy Laughlin rode behind a massive boulder, Lafe angled around the tree he was using for cover to check the draw. Cajun was putting pressure on the two riflemen who were trying to shoot along the side of the shoulder of earth.

Reacting in kind, Ruffner then shot over the top, showing himself from the shoulders up. Lafe quickly slammed the stock of his Winchester into position. Fire from Billy Laughlin splintered the tree by his ear. Lafe dropped but he wouldn't let himself be distracted. Crouching up, he sprang to the side, slid hard into the ground along his front, and leveled the rifle as Ruffner came up again. He lined his aim and the Winchester leapt in his hands. Ruffner flew back, red covering his face. Lafe crawled to the next tree and returned Billy's fire.

Phin put his revolver in its sheath as Jesse swung around to join his brother. He ran with legs doubled to his horse tearing at its tether, pulled his rifle, dashed for a near tree, and, facing the draw, left the Laughlins at the boulder for Lafe. Cajun was getting nowhere trading shots with Amos. Phin sprayed Claibourne's cover with relentless fire.

The slugs plowed the ground all about Amos. With the rifleman down, Cajun didn't hesitate. He tugged the reins around and, beating the black's flanks, sprinted back the way he had come, swinging around suddenly ten yards on. The horse reared and lunged up and over the rim. Cajun galloped for the trees.

The Laughlins were making their play. Billy rode out from behind the boulder, to the right, skirting the far side of the willows. Jesse came out to the left and headed toward the draw.

Billy fired twice at Lafe, keeping him low. Continuing on, he put Lafe out of position, caught between the gun and his cover. Billy emptied his chambers in a tight cluster, making Lafe scramble wildly for the other side of the tree.

Phin got no more return fire from Amos. He pivoted to see Jesse coming around to his side, cutting loose. The thin tree would do him little good. He took a chance. He grabbed his horse's reins and dragged him around for a shield, trying to work his carbine over the animal's neck. Jesse aimed for the horse and shot him three times. Trying to break away just as it was hit, the horse toppled in Phin's direction, pinning the detective's leg underneath.

Jesse had two targets. Phin was still partially shielded, and Lafe had his back to him. He went for Lafe. He got off one errant shot, then reined around to face Cajun Lee approaching the edge of the trees.

The outlaw pulled his second gun, rode toward Cajun's side, and opened up. Cajun snapped a shot with the Colt, spilled from the saddle, rolled over fast to the side of a tree, ducked under a ricocheted shot, spun around to the other side of the tree, and brought up his gun. The rider crossed by him. Cajun fired once and Laughlin threw up his hands and pitched back out of the saddle. His right foot caught in the stirrup and the big man jerked to a stop in mid-air as he reached the end of his slack. The horse dragged him bouncing along the ground for several yards.

Billy Laughlin held his fire for a beat, his eyes riveted on the man in the serape on the other side of the stand of trees. Renewed fire from Lafe brought him back into action and the sight of Cajun coming to take cover on his side forced his decision. With two guns shooting at Cajun he swerved his horse around and took off for the hills to the west. He made it out of range and rode out of sight.

Lafe rushed over to Phin and helped him pry the leg loose. The detective's leg had been straightened out when it was caught under the horse so none of the joints had been damaged. Cajun crept back over to the draw and made sure that Amos had also taken off. Most likely he had already gotten back to his horse and was on his way. Levi Ruffner was dead. Jesse Laughlin would be in just a few moments.

While bringing back his horse, Cajun was approached by Lafe. The chief detective looked at him with a hint of a smile.

"I guess me and Phin ought to thank you. That was some fast work you did."

Cajun ejected his spend shells and said he was just doing his job.

Lafe glanced back at Phin pulling off his saddle and said, "For someone who's just after the silver you sure seem to take the job seriously."

Cajun looked up and met the man's stare. He tried to figure out if there was an accusation hidden in the man's words. Lafe answered the unasked question.

"It was simple enough to tell. Some of us'll just take what we're paid and others are after the big stake. Even if I didn't find out from Joe Anson about the talk you had with him, I could still see you had big ideas. Phin might be in on it too, but it doesn't matter." He half-turned to walk back. "The way I see it, you'll do an even better job with that sort of money to shoot for. You sure as hell have so far." A glint came into his steely eyes as he added, "Just one thing. When this is all over, we're going to have ourselves a night up at Red Rock and you're going to buy."

"You got yourself a deal there, fella."

15

The three detectives took up Amos' trail. Billy was apparently taking a roundabout route and would probably lead them through a variety of evasive moves that only someone born to the area could know. Clearing their way through that sort of sign would eat up more time than they could afford.

With Phin taking Jesse's horse, they started off, each taking a turn riding along higher ground to sight any ambush. They found the spot where Amos had retrieved his horse on the other side of the ridge and followed the markings down a switchback. Along the way, Amos had pulled a trick of his own, leaving the detectives a false route that they weren't able to unravel until they found the hidden path through some thicket. The time they lost was crucial. When they reached the valley it was empty.

The grassy cove had only two approaches—the pass through the mountains to the north and the gorge to the southwest that split into two valleys further on. Billy, Amos, and Sol herded the last of the cattle down the pass and into the cove, circling the perimeter until the animals were settled. Billy drew up alongside Sol. He stared off intently as he spoke.

"Go get Johnny. Tell him what happened. Tell him we got the cattle in the cove but they're still after us and we got to move the cattle to Crispus Valley. We'll need two or three more men."

"Maybe we should just take 'em ourselves, Billy. Won't have to sit around and wait."

"Just do what I say. You'll get back before they reach us."

"He be at the ranch?"

"Yeah. Now get moving, goddamnit. We need those men to do it right."

"Watch how you talk to me, Billy. It wasn't me who said to go after those detectives."

Billy turned to him, his eyes flaring. He backhanded Sol across the face. "That was my brother they killed! You open your mouth again and I'll shoot you where you are!"

Sol's face reddened where he was hit but he didn't put a hand up to it. He returned his cousin's gaze sullenly and rode off through the gorge.

At the Claibourne place, he found Baehma, Josh, and Ave patching up the corral fence. He told them about the fight.

"Jesse and Levi were killed," he said. "It was the Cajun that got Jesse."

Baehma tightened his grip on the hammer in his right hand and flung it savagely at the fencing. He swore in a growl. Ave Laughlin's voice wavered slightly.

"That fella's been around too long."

"Well, we ain't doing any good standing around here," Baehma snapped.

"Well, I ain't the one who said I was taking care of him. You said that when my brother was still living."

137

Baehma spun toward Laughlin but no words came to him. The tense silence was broken by Sol. "Billy said we need more men to get the cattle clear."

Baehma told Josh and Ave to saddle up and sent Sol off to Gallino Station to round up Morgan Fleet and Tobey. Riding off with Josh and Ave, the outlaw chief began sizing up the sides as they stood now.

With Jesse and Levi Ruffner gone, that made it eight men including himself. And with Sol's bad shoulder making him little more than an errand boy, the number was better set at seven. Tolfane's range detectives numbered the same. Baehma found it hard to consider that even. His men were grumbling too much, to the extent that Ave was now sounding off. He didn't know how much he could depend on them in a pinch.

Topping a slope and swinging around for the down-trail, the three men saw the group of horsemen to their rear looking small in the distance as they rode along the arroyo. The group swerved to the side, masking themselves behind the line of cottonwood at the foot of the slope, but their intentions were clear.

"The Mexes," Josh said.

Baehma nodded. "They're sticking closer all the time."

It was then, at the sight of the Mexicans behind them, that Baehma saw what he had to do. He told Ave and Josh to go on ahead and join Billy with the cattle. He would clear their back-trail—after that he had plans of his own.

Baehma didn't think the Mexicans were much of a threat on their own but combined with the new losses, and with Tolfane's men closing in, it was clear that the time had come for new action. From one side or the other, maybe both, a showdown was in the making and Baehma was not content to fight it the way things stood.

Circling around to an overlooking bluff, the outlaw chief took to the ground with his rifle and took a few shots at the Mexicans as they started up the slope. His only hit was to the neck of a horse, but he had them distracted and scared enough to take after him. In a short time he had them winding through the hills. He left them there and doubled back, riding away from the high ground. He was headed for the telegraph office along the road below Gallino Station.

A little less than an hour later, Baehma walked the steeldust down the southern grade into Crispus Valley. The herd was already there. At the north end, Sol and Ave were covering the trail. The other five drifted toward Baehma as he reached the stock, Billy and Josh coming first.

"There wasn't any sign of them yet when we left the cove," Billy said. "They won't be getting around to here for some time."

Baehma waited for Morgan Fleet and Amos to come within hearing distance before he responded. He wanted an audience for when he took the initiative.

"Was it your idea to tangle with those detectives, Billy?"

The boyish face tightened, rage and humiliation somewhere behind it but only showing through briefly. "Yeah. It was me."

"No reason for it, Billy. You could've just

moved the cattle on. That's all you had to do!"

Billy darted a glance at Fleet and Amos stepping to his side, then looked down, his jaw clamped hard. Baehma shook his head loosely.

"God damn it, that was all you had to do. Now we got two more to bury. That's two less guns and now Tolfane's men know where to start looking because you led them in to the old hideaway. They won't be here for awhile, you're right about that, but they'll get around to it and then we'll have to move them again. And there'll be more times after that because these sons of bitches ain't quitting and they're shooting back now, you can all see that. So what the hell you think we're going to do now?"

There was no response at first. Josh then spoke up. "We're just gonna have to go at it with them. Sooner or later, might as well be sooner."

"You think that, huh? You think you boys can stand up to Tolfane's men? Don't look like it so far. Especially with the Mexes breathing down our necks. That won't make it no easier."

Josh answered as Tobey joined the group from the side and Sol and Ave approached from the other. "Hell, Johnny, we know all that. You got some ideas, tell it to us." Claibourne's face was getting ruddy with impatience but Baehma tried to ignore this.

"I got an idea, that's right. And maybe it'll be enough to get us through this because we sure as hell ain't doing it the way things are now." The outlaw chief swept the faces around him, careful to meet every look. "I know a couple of good men in San Miguel. I just sent a wire to tell them to ride down. They should be here in a day or two."

There was no sound except for the slow milling

of the cattle. Baehma could see the Claibournes and Laughlins passing secretive looks. Finally, he couldn't wait for them to speak up.

"These fellas know how to handle themselves, you can be sure of that. Tolfane's boys'll have their hands full when they try to mix it up with these—"

"Outsiders!"

Amos prodded his horse into the middle of the group. "Outsiders are coming in? Is that what we come to?"

"Hold on there, Johnny." The controlled urgency of Josh's voice put Amos off before he could get started. "Now you talk about what happened today and you say it shouldn't of happened and that we got ourselves in a hole and I'll say you're talking sense. But this is something else." He had a spread hand out and moved it as he talked, looking like he was keeping something in place. "Now you know there ain't been no outsiders with us since you and Morgan come a few years back. Everything we do is for the family and that's how it's always been."

Baehma tried to keep his voice matter-of-fact, as if dismissing a minor notion. "Morg and me were let in a few years ago because we could help the family. We need help now so we're bringing two or three more fellers in."

"I remember it different, Johnny, and Amos and Sol and Billy and Ave will tell you the same. You and Morg were let in because of one reason. The Old Man said you could be let in. Now the Old Man ain't around anymore and there ain't no one who can bring somebody in."

Nostrils flared and mouths were set hard, as Amos grasped the heavy gold cross. Johnny Baehma turned to Morgan Fleet. He had one hope of a place to start, with someone outside of the family.

"What do you say, Morg? We're in a fix here, everybody knows it. You see it's time to be reasonable, don't you?"

Morgan Fleet crossed his arms on his pommel and leaned forward pensively. "Seems to me, a couple more men with us is just goin' to mean the money's goin' to be spread out a little thinner."

"What the hell you talkin' about? Two men died today. Now we get two more. It comes out the same."

"I know better than that, Johnny. It was a Laughlin that died and an outsider. Laughlins get the same cut to split amongst themselves no matter what. That means it's the outsiders who get shaved and that's me."

"Me too," Tobey said thinly.

Baehma felt the blood rushing to his face, his scalp prickling. He wanted to pistol whip the next man who talked and gun down the first man who'd object. Only through force of will did he hold himself back. He knew he was walking on unsteady ground and whatever he did he had to win these men over. As useless as they would be without him to tell them what to do, without them he was just another lone wolf gunman. Ave Laughlin was now putting in his say.

"And what are these new fellas gettin'? Maybe they're gettin' more than the rest of us because you say they're so special."

"It ain't going to be nothing like that, Ave. You should know me better than that. You all do. I've always took care of you. And I've always done what the Old Man told me I should do because he was like a father to me! And now I'm also doing what the Old Man would've wanted! Two of us were killed today, a Laughlin and Levi Ruffner who knew you all since he was knee-high to a grasshopper. What I'm trying to do is set things right by them and this is the only way I can do it."

Ave worked his pursed lips agitatedly. "It ain't just Jesse and Levi. There's Ike and Aaron and Nick. And Josh here was hobblin' around and Sol can't much use his left arm. It was you who was talkin' it up, Johnny, about doin' something about it."

Sol stood in his stirrups. "And after the beaners shot up the station we wanted to get even the only way we can and you got us swiping cattle instead."

"Our ways have got twisted," Amos rasped. "We've been strayin' off the path. The Lord has looked down kindly on us and given us this land out of the desert because it has to be ours and no one else's. We have to keep this land clean of any others and when others trifle with us we must give them the worst."

"That's what I intend to do," said Baehma. "We're going to make them pay. We're just going to do it a different way."

Looking to the others, Josh said, "The Old Man didn't need no one to take care of things. He didn't even need us when he was riled enough. Like when that trooper was passing through and said he had to take some fresh horses from us for his men and he didn't have no money. They never did find him."

"Amen, brother."

"You're forgetting something, ain't you?" Baehma paused, rankled that he was forced to

143

match stories. "That night at Gallino Station with the greasers all around, I don't recall asking you boys for anything. As a matter of fact, if it wasn't for those beaners I dropped, you might still be there."

Josh spoke the words under his breath, without emphasis, for they didn't need any. "Mexes," he said. "Nobody counts them."

"That is the way it is for certain, brother. The Old Man led us here and would just sweep them aside as you would any heathen." Amos' voice found its ranting edge, gathering strength as he went. "There weren't nothing he would let pass when it came to his people. And when it came to the test, when it was white men who came against our own, his vengeance was terrible swift. He would strike them down, every last one of them. No white man could stand against him when he had vengeance in him. Not a single one—"

At times the Sloan bunch listened to Amos just to humor him, but that wasn't the case as he continued now. The touched man had them soaking up every word. Baehma could only keep quiet with the rest. He noticed Billy Laughlin watching his cousin keenly, his eyes about to well. There was no interrupting Amos when he had the family in his sway.

Only one choice was open to Baehma. He wasn't going to change his mind about the new men. He needed more guns and he wanted someone to side with him against whoever had trailed him to the Old Man's place and, most importantly, he wasn't about to back down. He would have to do something else to win back his men's confidence.

Amos now whipped the thick cross from around

144

his neck and repeatedly swung it down in front of him. "He would strike them down! The trooper who tried to take our stock, he struck him down! The drifter who took the money from our gaming table, he struck him down! The squatter who tried pushing us from our water-hole—"

When the Old Man first made Johnny Baehma his chief lieutenant, the Claibournes and Laughlins grumbled then also, making it very plain what they thought of the newcomer giving them orders. The Old Man could have put an end to it with just a word, but he stood back and let Johnny fend for himself. Then one night while on a drinking spree in Sloan, Baehma gunned down the sheriff. No one questioned him after that and when the Old Man was killed he took over without objection. The fact that the sheriff's back was turned made absolutely no difference.

Later in the day, Josh and Tobey were left to keep watch on the cattle and the rest took off for either Sloan or Gallino Station. Baehma told Billy to come with him into town. They talked to Schliessen at the store and asked him when he thought some of Tolfane's men would be coming in to buy provisions, and were told that a shipment of ammunition had come in that afternoon and that two or three of them would be coming in tonight to pick it up. Baehma made his plans.

16

The night was blustery, the chill in the air bringing the first signal of the break between seasons. With jacket collars turned up, Lafe Jenkins, Heck Buel, and Ray Pence rode deliberately into Sloan with a pack horse trailing. From the far end of the road came a spurt of loud voices. They came from the cantina and Lafe judged there were two, maybe three of them. The three detectives passed the pinewood shack, seeing the light from inside but hearing no sound. Stopping on the north side of the store, away from the cantina, they loose-tied the horses to the rail and Heck Buel left the other two to go inside for the provisions.

Lafe and Pence stationed themselves at the store's front corner, raking the street in both directions. In all, the transaction would take only a couple of minutes and the likelihood of a run-in with drunken outlaws was slim, but Lafe had insisted on two extra men for insurance. Buel had been inside for thirty seconds when the door of the shack across the way was flung open and Billy Laughlin strode out. The woman's pleading could be heard even before she rushed out the door. She clung to Billy's sleeve, saying "No, Billy, no! Please, no!" It was Anna, the plump Mexican whore who stayed with the Sloan bunch from time to time.

Billy yanked his arm free of her hold and continued on to his horse at the side of the shack. He walked at a sneering, unhurried pace, then turned abruptly to see the two detectives by the store. He quickened his step, shoved the whore aside, mounted up and swung the animal around to take off to the north at a long lope, lifting to a gallop once out of town. The woman ran up the street after him, then dropped to her knees, sobbing loudly.

Lafe told Pence to stay put and walked out into the street to the woman's side.

"What's going on? What'd he do?"

"He took it from me," she said between tearful heaves.

"Took what?"

She looked up at him pitifully. "The cross from my mother. I tol' him is gold and he took it from me. I should never tell him. My mother she give it to me and is gone." The last words were muffled as she dropped her face to her hands.

Lafe watched the whore uncomfortably. He stared off in the direction Laughlin had ridden off into and said, "Like to do something about it but I've got other business. Maybe one of his friends can get it back for you. He might listen to them."

He turned to leave but stopped short as Anna grabbed a pants leg. "You get it for me, please. Go now, he not far yet." The large eyes in the round face looked up at him beseechingly.

"I told you, I got business. I don't even know where he went. He could be anywhere."

"No, please, you can find him! He say he go to look after the ganado. You know where is that, yes?''

Lafe leaned forward. ''The cattle?''

''Sí. Ganado.''

She continued pleading as Lafe quickly turned it over in his mind. He glanced back at Pence and saw he was still waiting for Buel. The town was quiet enough. Two men could bring back the ammunition as well as three. If he was going to try it he would have to go now and by himself. He couldn't risk taking another man from the shipment.

''I'll go,'' he said.

He hurried back to the store, told Pence what he was up to, saddled up and rode hard to the north.

There was light enough to follow the sign at a canter. A few miles outside of town he saw that Laughlin had swung to the left and taken off in a southwesterly direction. At Berino Mesa he had shifted toward the south, past a rock-sided pass through a hollow.

Lafe entered the pass, relishing the protection from the harsh wind, considering Billy's route. It seemed he might be skirting around the rough passage of Spider Pass, which would probably cut down on time. In another half hour Lafe would slow down his gait and maybe camp till the outlaws made their next change in shift rather than go in blind. He was reaching the end of the pass when a voice cut through the whistling of wind through rocks. ''Jenkins.''

Lafe drew his gun, spun around, and desperately keened the night. Twin streaks of light stabbed through the dark. The earth wrenched away from beneath him and he saw the sky flash by in a sudden arc. Crushed to the ground, his mind feverishly

148

tried recalling if he'd heard the two blasts. Then there was blackness.

There was no reason to wait for any sign of movement. Johnny Baehma got up from behind the rock, collected his horse at the opening of the pass and rode off to meet Margarita at the ranch.

They found him the next morning.

Not getting any word from Lafe by sunup, the range detectives rode into Sloan and followed his trail from there. At the far side of the pass through the rocky hollow they saw him stretched out on his back. Judging from the markings, he'd been thrown about seven feet from where he had been sitting on his horse. The full eighteen buckshot from a double-barrelled shotgun had ripped through him just below the chest wall. Lafe was just about cut in two.

The silence lasted a long time as the six men stood circled about the body. Cajun stared at the dead man's face. The lips were pulled back in a fixed, speechless grimace. Cajun's throat constricted, he felt his vision lose focus for a moment. He turned and slowly walked away.

Stuffing his hands into his pockets, Ray Pence scanned the faces about him and was the first to speak. "Saw some cottonwood by the opening back there. Could make a litter from that to take him back in."

There was another beat of quiet before Charley Benton answered. "You say it was that Mex whore what sent him along?"

"She's the one. Right after Billy Laughlin lit out."

"Half of us can make the litter," Phin said.

"The rest can go to Sloan and see which one put her up to it."

"Fair enough," Benton replied. "But who says who gets the chance to go to Sloan?"

"No sense in standing around jawing about it. We'll have to draw straws or such. Ain't no other way to—"

The fast drum on horse hoofs turned them all around. Toward the other end of the pass, Cajun Lee galloped away on his black. He swept around the last line of rock and turned out of view, headed for Sloan. The other detectives watched without speaking for several moments.

Pence tilted his hat back on his head. "I think we'll get the litter done faster if we all just pitch in at once. What do you say?"

17

When he saw Baehma come through the door, Miles Forber left his stocking chores at the front of the store and found an excuse to wander to the room in the back. It was understood between the partners that whenever the outlaw chief came in it would be Schliessen that waited on him. The understanding had been reached on a mutual basis.

Forber was particularly thankful for the arrangement on this day. Through the back door, he watched Schliessen meet the outlaw at the counter, almost feeling sorry for the fool for having been so greedy.

"I'll be needing some cartridges," Baehma said. "Give me a couple of boxes."

Schliessen automatically started for the rack against the side wall, then stopped himself, turning to Baehma, the pinched face above Schliessen's thick body drawn anxiously.

"Spit it out, Schliess. What is it?"

"That feller with Tolfane, the one with the serape. He was around this morning, asking about the shooting last night. He talked to Anna."

Baehma considered the merchant intently but calmly. "When was this?" he asked.

"A couple hours ago. Around nine o'clock."

"You know what Anna told him?"

151

Schliessen looked down at the bare wood plank counter and slowly gripped its edge. "He knows."

"Where'd he go from here?"

"Looked like he was off for the station. Anna couldn't tell him where you were so he's making the rounds." He wiped his hand across his pants and added, "Seems like him and Jenkins were pretty friendly."

Baehma nodded and asked if that was all. Disappointed with the outlaw's casualness, Schliessen said that it was.

"All right then. Get me those cartridges."

Schliessen shuffled to the rack and brought back the two boxes of .44's. Pocketing them and turning to leave, Baehma said to put it on his credit.

"Wait a minute, Johnny." The outlaw half-turned to him. "I think he knows that I told you about the detectives coming in for the ammunition."

"Know that for a fact?"

"Anna said she didn't tell him but she sure was talking to him for a long time. He's got to know."

"Well, maybe he does."

The merchant's voice crackled with desperation. "He might be coming for me, Johnny. Sooner or later. Hell, what am I supposed to do? I hear he's as fast as you are."

"What the hell do you expect me to do about that?"

"Couldn't you leave somebody here just in case? Billy maybe?"

"No." The outlaw started for the door.

"Johnny, I helped you out! I helped you plenty of times!"

Baehma faced him slowly and leveled a hard

stare at him. "You got paid for it. You always got paid, so quit belly-achin'. Everyone takes their chances."

When the outlaw was out the door, Schliessen walked numbly to the back.

Outside, Baehma tightened the cinch on his saddle and absently stroked the steeldust's neck. He had expected the detectives to try to strike back but he hadn't considered the possibility of it being a matter between him and the Cajun. The situation demanded a new approach.

The plan came to him quickly, with little effort or haste. He rode off to the west. At the Claibourne ranch he told the boys he had a lot of riding to do and his quarter horse needed a breather. Taking a buckskin mare from the corral, he mounted up with a spare saddle and, leaving the steeldust in the front as a decoy, left for the telegraph office to see if any response had come from San Miguel.

Baehma figured he could stay out of sight at a ranch to the south. The next day he would come back to see how things stood. He didn't consider himself a cowardly man, but neither was he one to take chances if he didn't have to. If the fight came to him, there would be one hell of a fight, but until then or that time when he made his own terms, he would play it safe.

Cajun got an open view of the Claibourne place from the top of one of the hills off to the southeast. Three men were in the corral on the opposite side of the house, adding supports to the fencing. They were Amos and Josh Claibourne and Billy Laughlin. Cajun would have moved on except for the steeldust hitched in front with the two other saddled horses.

He left the black picketed in a cove of trees a hundred yards from the ranch house and, taking a second Colt from his saddle bag and stuffing it in the front of his gun belt with the butt to the right, he stole for the corral, keeping the house in between for cover. Halfway across the clearing he stopped behind a mound to check the windows. No sign of anyone who could spot him from inside. He moved the rest of the distance in a crouch, came up to the side of the house, and crept around to the corner across from the corral, some ten feet away. He pulled the gun from its holster and dashed for the corral's near entrance, swinging around inside and backing against the close slat fencing for cover.

"There's a gun on you," he hissed.

The three men froze, then turned slowly in his direction. They all wore gun belts but no suggestion of a move was made. Billy straightened from his work at the base of the fence to face Cajun squarely.

"All right," Cajun said. "Fast and quiet. Is Baehma inside?" The three men exchanged glances. "I said, fast." When Billy opened his mouth, Cajun added, "And keep it down."

"There ain't nobody inside."

Cajun pointed the gun at Amos and Josh. "You two say that also?"

"Nobody's in there," said Josh.

Before telling them to drop their guns, which could signal someone in the house, Cajun ordered Billy to call Baehma outside.

"You want me to holler for him?" Billy laughed dryly. "I'm going to feel pretty foolish calling for somebody that ain't there."

"Well, I'd feel even more foolish if I didn't make you do it."

Laughlin called out several times before Cajun was satisfied. He straightened up from the cover of the fence and stepped forward. "His horse is here. When did he leave?"

"Hour or two ago."

"Where did he go?"

"How the hell should I know? It ain't my business to keep tabs on him." As Billy met the gray-eyed stare, the thoughts that had come to him when he first saw that the Cajun had the drop now took hold of him. There was Nick and Jesse to pay for. "Why don't you put that gun away?" he said. "You afraid someone might beat you?"

"I've got a better idea. I don't have any business here, but I'm not about to ride away with three guns at my back. Toss them down."

Reluctantly, Josh pulled his revolver.

Without taking his eyes from Cajun, Billy said, "You going to let him talk you out of it so easy?"

"Slow down, Billy," Josh advised. "We ain't getting anywhere like this."

"There's three of us, Josh."

"Now's not the time."

Josh dropped the gun to the ground. Amos glanced unsurely at the two beside him, then followed Josh's example.

Cajun said, "Your turn now, Billy."

"You want it, you're going to have to take it away from me."

Cajun blew out a tired breath. Anna had told him that Laughlin was part of last night's ambush, but he didn't want to waste time with the young

155

man. It was Baehma that he wanted. "You're just dragging this out, Billy. Either you drop it or I take it. That's the only two ways it's going to be. Won't make much difference in the end, will it?"

"It could be another way too, mister. You put it away and we can settle this straight-up."

Cajun took another step forward, coming to within ten feet of Laughlin. "This is the last time I'll say it. Take it out with your fingers and drop it."

Maybe Johnny will make himself scarce, thought Billy, but not me. "I hear you're really something with that Colt of yours, mister. But I ain't seen that much. You did some fast thinking the other day, but the shooting wasn't nothing I ain't seen before."

Josh and Amos moved slowly to the side, but Cajun could see they kept within reaching distance of their guns on the ground. He walked towards Billy, who started up again.

"Maybe you ought to know something, mister. When you're friend got gut-shot last night, I was the one who set him up." Cajun came to a stop five feet away. "If it wasn't for me, it wouldn't't've happened. I led him right to it, the poor shit."

Cajun could feel the blood pumping through his neck, the cords of the neck sticking out. He knew he wouldn't get any closer to the man. Slowly, and as evenly as could he said, "I knew you were a part of it, Billy. But I didn't know you'd stand there like that and brag about it. That makes you just that much lower."

Cajun backed off three deliberate paces and, shifting the front of his serape over his left shoulder, holstered his gun. "Get to work, boy. If you want it that bad."

The two men stood motionless for a space of time frozen in the concentration of the moment. Amos and Josh stood intently, eyeing both men as well as their dropped weapons. It could have been a few seconds or a little more. Then Billy's wrist twisted down.

The black Colt jumped from its holster and roared. The slug crashed through Billy's breast bone, sending him back a foot. After the slightest tortured hesitation, Laughlin crooked his gun arm up. Cajun's Colt barked twice more and the outlaw spun back with the first and barrelled into the fence behind with the next, slinking down with his arms and legs splayed at unnatural angles.

Josh bent a knee, angled his right hand down, then suddenly stopped. In a blurred rounded motion, Cajun border-shifted the Colt to his left hand and, with his right, pulled the spare gun from his belt, cocked and aimed at Josh. The first revolver, with its two remaining rounds, was leveled at Amos. Josh stood hunched over, his hand still a foot and a half from his hardware. Amos took an involuntary step back. Josh stood up slowly, his hands hanging loosely at his sides. He glanced back at his cousin, heaped in the dirt at the base of the fence, the wide, empty eyes staring back at him.

Cajun picked up the two guns and put one in his holster, the other in his belt. "I'll leave these off when I get back to my horse." He turned on his heels and headed back the way he had come, around the back of the house. He stopped at the corner, remembering a bit of conversation from some time before. Amos and Josh watched quizzically as he crossed to the front of the house, turned out of view, and then came back to the corral, leading the gray steeldust by the reins.

Cajun swung into the saddle and faced the two Claibournes. "I got a message for Johnny. Tell him I came for him. Tell him he can come to get his horse back anytime."

He reined around and started for the cove of trees, kneeing the thick-muscled animal into a long, fast lope.

The next morning Baehma returned to the ranch and was told of what had happened to Billy and given the message from Cajun.

There were no recriminations for his not having been around when it happened. Lafe's death had at least brought him the respect of silence. But there would be no wasting time either. Johnny Baehma would settle accounts and it would be on his terms. His decision cost him bitter irritation but something had to be done.

That afternoon Baehma rode into Sloan and found Schliessen in the store, packing things for a short trip west "for his health." Baehma told him there was one thing for him to do before leaving. "You're going to get on your buckboard and ride up to the Tolfance place. Tell the son of a bitch I want to talk."

18

Tolfane had heard of the Old Man's place but had never really expected to find out where in the western hills it was located. That night he was to learn the secret.

Following the directions given him by Schliessen, the rancher reined his horse around the shelf at the base of the high ground and stopped for the wait. He huddled against the cooling night air for ten minutes before hearing his name called. Johnny Baehma appeared at his side, leading the buckskin out of a passage between the rocks. Without a word, Baehma mounted and led the way along the edge of the hills. After a mile they turned for the upward climb, following a maze-like trail that Tolfane strained to remember.

Coming down the lip into the secluded hollow, the outlaw chief swung off the horse, hitched it, and waited for Tolfane to do the same and find a seat on a log before he started to talk.

He said, "It's time we make ourselves a deal."

Tolfane stretched out his legs and crossed them leisurely. "What kind of deal, Johnny?"

The outlaw bristled at the silver-haired man's confidence. All the more so because the rancher had every reason to act that way. "You know damn well what kind. The deal we been fighting over all this time."

"Well, Johnny, you know the only kind of deal I would make. Correct me if I'm wrong, and I want you to understand that I mean no offense by this, but it seems to me that you're giving in. Am I right?"

Baehma's jaw tightened, holding back all the resentment that he knew would do him no good now. He moved over to the side of the grave, turning away from Tolfane. "You get a third. Just like the way it was before."

Tolfane came to his feet and strolled in the outlaw's direction, unable to suppress the quiet smile of satisfaction. "I'll tell you, Johnny, when I saw the Louisiana man come back to the ranch yesterday with that fine quarter horse of yours, I had a feeling you might decide to come around. I believe what they say. I think he is as fast as you are."

"Enough," Baehma snapped, wheeling to face the rancher. "My reasons are none of your concern. I'm telling you I'll let you have a third."

"All right, then, we'll talk business. Like you said, a third is what I received before but all this fighting has been a great drain on me. I think that at this point, a bonus of some kind would be in order, as a way of compensation."

"Don't stretch it, Tolfane. I've still got the guns on my side and I've got two more coming in and if it's the drain you don't like we can still give you a lot more. I'm doing this just to make things easier for the both of us."

"You've got the guns, do you? It seems to me I've heard that before. About six months ago I think it was. 'Don't tell me what to do,' you said.

'All you do is stash the cattle and set up a buyer. We have the guns.' That's when you came up with the bright idea of cutting me down to one quarter and now you got me here to talk because your fighters aren't holding up so well.''

"There's a few things I still haven't tried, Tolfane. If you want, we can keep at it for awhile and see what we can do to each other but I don't think that's going to do either of us any good. Especially when we can work something out now.''

"Perhaps you have a point. I think I'm willing to forget the compensation for now if it seems we can come to a worthwhile agreement.''

"There's the Mex cattle. We can start with that. A fair amount of money can come from that if you want it.''

Tolfane took only a moment to think about it. "I want it.''

"You find someone who wants to buy and we'll bring it over to where you want to hide them. Just like it was before.''

"That part sounds fair enough. Am I to believe that that is the whole bargain?''

"No, you're not.''

"I thought it was a little quick. What else is there?''

"Your detectives have got to go.''

Tolfane paced off, then turned back. "They are the only real insurance I have. How am I to know I won't need them?''

"You can hold on to them for awhile until you see that things are all right. You can get rid of them one at a time if you want to do it like that. But one way or the other, they go. Me and the boys are going to be the only real fighting men around

161

here."

The rancher was slow to answer.

"Which is it going to be?" Baehma demanded. "The detectives or the cattle?"

The outlaw's glower made Tolfane flinch inside. On the outside, he slipped his hands into his coat pockets, and hoping he appeared calculating. "I suppose you are right. It'll have to be the cattle. I don't have to pay them wages. I will take you up on dismissing them gradually, though. I have to take that precaution at least."

"No more than a month. After that, they're gone."

"I suppose I can go along with that." He stepped forward and extended his right hand. "Does that make the deal?"

Baehma stared at the outstretched hand, his own on his gun belt. "There's just one more thing."

"And what would that be?"

"I want the Cajun. You set him up and we take care of it."

"He's my best shootist, Johnny. I may need him after all."

"In another month you won't need him at all. You serve him up or there's no deal."

Tolfane brought his right hand up and lightly stroked his lower lip, seeing his own plans taken shape. He glanced around the clearing, taking a moment to peer into the blackness of the cave. "I think I can agree to that. But there has to be one condition."

"And what would that be?"

"I'll set him up, but I may want to send someone along with him, for my own reasons. Do you think you can handle two as well as one?"

Baehma looked at him oddly, but could see no reason to be suspicious. "That's all? Just adding an extra man?"

"That's all."

"I think we got a deal."

Baehma stuck out his large hand and they shook on it. Tolfane casually motioned toward the cave.

"This is quite a secret spot you have here. It must be pleasant to have a place all to your own, to be able to shut yourself off from everyone else."

The outlaw narrowed his eyes doubtfully. "I like it."

"Especially for a meeting like this. You wouldn't want other people spying on you, not even your own men. You can't let them know everything."

"What the hell you getting at, Tolfane?"

"Why, nothing. Nothing at all to get upset at." He darted a glance at the cave, then turned nervous under Baehma's scrutiny. "Really, Johnny, all I was saying was that you told me to come here because you didn't want your men to happen to see you talking to me. They might get the wrong idea—think that you were selling out or something."

Baehma felt like grabbing him by the neck and shaking him and telling him not to think so much, but there was too much riding on Tolfane's cooperation. "That's right," he said. "I don't have nothing to hide."

"No one's saying you're hiding anything, Johnny."

"It's just that my men don't understand these things." He took the rancher's elbow and slowly turned him away from the cave. "I've got to tell

163

them you gave in because that's all they understand. They don't know business."

"Of course. Anyone can see that. It's your affair, not mine. I want it to be understood, Johnny,
that all I'm concerned about is my end of the thing.
It's just business between you and me and whatever
your reasons are for keeping this place a secret are
completely your affair. At this point, we shouldn't
let anything interfere with our deal."

Baehma eyed the rancher without trust, but
chose to change the subject. "We've got some
business right now. Like, what do we do about the
Cajun tomorrow?"

They talked over the next day's plans and agreed
upon the time and the place. When he left, Tolfane
said he remembered the route and didn't need a
guide for the way down. Baehma glared at the
rancher's back as he rode into the darkness. He
then went into the cave.

Behind the spine of rock leading up the slope,
Phin walked in place and rubbed his hands to keep
warm. Thoughts of what should be laying before
him also helped to fight the chill. From the other
side of the rock he heard the horse approaching. In
another minute Tolfane came into view, drawing
up across from the detective, still in the open. He
adjusted the scarf around his neck and face and
spoke while keeping eyes straight ahead.

"Wait till I round the end of the hills. That's
when he'll see that I'm on my way. If I guess right,
he should be coming down carrying a sack or chest
or the like. I want you to follow him and find out
where he takes it. You can report what you find out
in the morning. I should be asleep by the time you

return tonight.''

He buttoned the top of his coat and rode on. Phin watched him go with a thin smile on his face. Thinks I don't know what it is, Phin thought. If only the old bastard knew!

After the rancher turned out of view, the detective stepped on to his horse and positioned himself against the wall of rock, next to a fissure that gave him a line of sight along the edge of the range. Twenty minutes later, he saw the distant figure of Johnny Baehma ride out of the foothills. Resting on the saddle in front of the outlaw was a dark bulge that looked like a filled sack. Phin watched him walk the horse for half a mile along the level and, swinging out from his cover and keeping to the shadows of the range, started the slow trailing.

Keeping his distance, the detective followed the path that swung wide of the Claibourne ranch and veered north to the wagon road. The markings turned east on the road, making Baehma's destination clear. If he kept up this distance, Phin knew he might arrive too late to see where the loot would be stashed. He reined off the road and took off at a good clip in a direct line with Sloan.

A hundred yards to the west of town, he stationed himself behind a hillock. Presently, Baehma came up the road and passed the unlit shack. Looking through his spy glass, Phin watched him rein in behind the old sheriff's office, do his work amongst the rubble and lead his horse down the road to go into the cantina and join his friends. Phin set out for the Tolfane place, the warming thoughts coming back to him.

Past one o'clock in the morning, he found the ranch dark and perfectly still. He left his horse in the stable and circled around to the back of the building to begin his last wait for the night.

He heard the footsteps come lightly along the ground, felt his limbs charge with anticipation and, when Mrs. Tolfane finally appeared around the corner, the words blurted from his mouth in an urgent rasp.

"I found the silver."

He beamed as he watched her react and, before she could respond, grabbed her around the waist.

"Now we've got it!" he said.

He clutched her close and the lady fended him off, playfully giggling.

At the master bedroom window, Tolfane stood rigidly in his nightclothes and robe, listening to the soft ripple of laughter coming across the close night air. A mordant smile passed across his lips.

Cajun Lee would have company tomorrow.

19

The Bittner boy had chanced upon the tracks just north of Spider Pass, Tolfane said. He had been out hunting in the mountains and had come upon the sign of beeves moving to the south. After talking to his father, he'd decided that the information could be of use to Tolfane. Cajun and Phin had gotten the call to check up on the story.

With Lafe's murder still on his mind, Cajun didn't make any mention of new tactics for finding the silver while riding off with Phin. Although he was grateful for the silence, he found it peculiar that his partner also didn't bring up the subject. He considered starting the talk in order to try gleaning what was on the other man's mind but instead came to the conclusion that he could do without Phin's conversation for the time being. It could wait till their business at the Bittner place was finished.

An hour's ride from the ranch brought them to Sandoval Ravine. It was the only practical route to their destination, any other taking them many miles out of the way. The sides were steep and rutted and spotted with half unearthed boulders. On approaching the opening, Cajun had his usual misgivings about entering any stretch of land so well covered from above and so vulnerable below.

But he was anxious to be done with this chore and to use the day for more important matters. The two detectives moved down the grade toward the ravine.

At the crest of the hill, Diego Robles squatted and waited for his man to return. With his binoculars he swept the jagged rim of the ravine before him but could not make out anyone there.

He had heard about the fight between the Tolfane men and members of the Sloan bunch by Ransum Draw. He knew that Baehma's men had to move the cattle and that the next day Billy Laughlin had been killed by the Cajun. With that sort of trouble on their hands, the outlaws stood a fair chance of moving the cattle again some time soon and Robles intended to be near when it happened. At first light that morning, he and his men had picked up the trail of Baehma's group of five by the Claibourne place and had come to this standstill a little less than an hour ago.

At first, when the outlaws had disappeared below the rim, Robles had fretted that Baehma had tumbled to the back-trailers and was setting a trap, but he was quick to regain his head and realize that there had been no way for him to be discovered. As the goings-on of the past few days had become more and more desperate, Robles was finding more resources at his command and more of the old skills coming back to him. No, there had been no mistakes this time. This was something else at work. But what?

Camilo Lucero and Fernando left the two others with the horses and crept up the slope to their jefe's side.

"No sign of Urbina?" Lucero asked.

"He won't be long. He's just being cautious."

"Cautious!" Fernando spat out the word. "The time has come and gone for being cautious."

"What would you do, Fernando? Ride in, just like that?"

"They must be just sitting there. Just waiting there. We could take them."

"You think they are waiting? What are they waiting for?"

"I don't know. What does it matter?"

Struggling with impatience, Robles kept his voice even. "It could matter a great deal. What if they are waiting for more men from Sloan?"

Fernando looked away, his hand pawing the dust restlessly.

"How much more can we wait?" said Lucero. "I have lost one brother and another still hasn't healed from his wound. We can leave the cattle for later. We have accounts to settle."

"Do you think I have forgotten, Camilo? And do you think I have forgotten about Luisa? When the cattle were taken I still wanted blood, but I put that aside because I knew that others couldn't live without the stock. That was the only thing to do. So don't tell me about settling accounts."

Robles suddenly turned away from the two. He realized he hadn't even allowed himself to think of Luisa for the past few days and now the mere mention of her name unleashed a violent rage that made him doubt the logic of his words.

"We are six," Fernando said, "and they are only five. I say—no more waiting."

Robles tried braking the flood of thoughts. "We had them outnumbered at Gallino Station also," he said.

"That was different. Lopez was a fool."

"And who's going to be the fool this time? I know it is not going to be me, Fernando." Robles stared off blindly toward the rim.

Sullen and unsatisfied, Fernando didn't bother with a response. The hill became quiet. To the left they saw Urbina climb out of the gully and jog across the short flat piece into the hills. The six Mexicans met by the horses.

"They are below the rim," Urbina said. "Their horses are off to the side and they are hiding with their rifles out. Two of Tolfane's men just came into the ravine. It's the two that had Fleet the other day."

"An ambush," said Lucero. "They can have the two pigs. Maybe we can trap Baehma when he leads his men out."

Robles put off Lucero with a motion of his hand, turning to Urbina. "How far off are the Tolfane men from the rifles?"

"They should come abreast of them in a minute or two."

Fernando asked if they were going to take action and do what Lucero suggested. Stepping to his pinto, Robles weighed the notion that had just occurred to him.

Soon after riding into the ravine, Cajun's misgivings were gripped by an undefined instinct that hardened them into a gnawing dread. He couldn't tag it to even the faintest sound or scent or anything tangible, which made him suspicious of even the uneasiness itself. He glanced at Phin, saw the man's vacant expression take on an intent cast.

170

They raked the slopes on both sides. Cajun swiveled in the saddle and his breath caught. Up on the left he glimpsed the flash of light on gun metal. In the span of an instant he placed the position of the gun, judged the riding time to either end of the gorge, became aware of his scalp beaded with sweat, and realized that he was pegged for dead.

"This way," he yelled and spun his black around in the direction they had come. Phin had his horse turned when the fire burst down on them.

Bullets whined past them, scattered the dirt below, bounced shrilly off rock, echoed deafeningly in their ears. Cajun looked frantically for cover and could find nothing. A slug tore through his serape. Another seared across his collar bone. He swung viciously around and broke for the other way out, hoping to split the fire. He beat the flanks, the pelting barrage still with him, and plunged ahead to find no cover in that direction either.

He whipped the Spencer from its sheath, jerking it to cock and firing with one hand up the slope. Three times he fired and then moved to the base of the gunmen's slope to cut down their angle.

Across the ravine's floor, he saw Phin's new, untried chestnut rear violently. Phin was thrown. As he hit the ground, Cajun bolted toward him. Phin emptied the chambers of his revolver waiting for his help and, as the black slowed alongside, grabbed the outstretched arm and swung aboard.

Handing the other man his rifle, Cajun pulled his Colt, charged for a distant exit in a zig-zag pattern, and saw a Sloan man slip down to closer cover. In a sharpened, heightened instant he concentrated and anticipated the next movement on

171

the slope and how he could take one of the bastards with him. Then the gunfire multiplied to an overwhelming din.

Cajun rode on for ten yards, felt Phin tugging on the back of his serape and wheeled abruptly to a stop. The space about them was suddenly free of gunfire.

Through the swirl of dust, Cajun peered upward and saw the Sloan men shooting across the width of the slope. Firing upon them from above and to the side were the Mexicans. Out of position, the outlaws hurried toward the horses on the right, returning fire as they went. Cajun and Phin took off for the left.

Nearing the ravine's end, they came across the chestnut trotting off in confusion. Phin jumped from the saddle and cornered the animal, then mounted it and raced after Cajun, taking to the open ground. The firing from the slope continued, thinning slowly. The detectives circled around, working upslope, and in a few minutes reached the Mexicans' position at the rim. Robles' men shot sporadically at the outlaws receding toward the hills, chasing them more than aiming for the kill. When Baehma's bunch was hidden by the terrain, Robles turned to face the detectives walking their horses towards him. The look on the detectives' faces was as quizzical as it was thankful. The Mexican watched them with his jaw set firm and a glint in his dark eyes. Phin was the first to speak.

"Shit, I'd never thought I'd be thanking you."

Robles motioned to the hills. "They may try coming back. We'll take you to a safe place." He ordered his men to their horses picketed in the gully and the group was soon on its way around the

172

ravine, heading into the east.

In a box canyon about five miles away they came to a run-down shack. Dismounting in front, Cajun felt his blood now rushing at a slower rate and his mind clear for questions. Robles sat down in the doorway and began filling his pipe. The other Mexicans clustered nearby, giving the two gringos inscrutable looks which, it seemed to Cajun, were not meant to conceal friendliness.

The jefe said, "I don't think they know of this place. We'll be able to stay for awhile."

"We're obliged for what you did," started Cajun, "but I hope you won't mind me asking you something."

"I'd be disappointed if you didn't."

"All right then. The last time we ran into you, you considered killing us. Why'd you save us now?"

"I'll be frank with you, sir. We need someone like you and your friend to help us. I'm hoping you might consider that now."

"Help you against Baehma?"

Robles nodded.

"Why should we?"

"We can offer you something. Not much, but something. If you help us fight and find the cattle, we probably could give you a hundred dollars apiece. Maybe more."

"Shoot," Phin said, "we make fifty more than that a month with Tolfane. You've got to be funnin' us."

Cajun turned to him. "We made that much with Tolfane."

"How you mean, Cajun?"

"We're not working for Tolfane any more. He

173

was the only one who knew about us going to the Bittner place. He set us up."

Phin took in the thought for a moment, then said, "What'd he set you up for?" His tone was accusing.

"I see you're not wondering about yourself. Maybe you better tell me something, partner."

The two men locked stares. Phin's surliness soon gave way to confusion. Almost to himself, he said, "Somebody's got some telling to do, that's for sure."

Robles got up and stepped towards the two Anglos. "Whatever Tolfane has done to you is your business. But, for me, one thing is clear. You are not Tolfane men anymore and that means you could work for us as well as anyone."

"I'm sorry, mister," Cajun said. "You saved our lives and we thank you for it but that doesn't mean we have to throw them away in this war of yours."

"But you'd be doing the right thing. With you we could clean out this territory. Think of that. And if that's not important to you, think of this. After this is done, you would be famous fighting men. Mucho hombres. When people know you like that, there can be money in it for you. A big man gets a big price."

"The answer's still the same. Phin can speak for himself, but I don't risk my neck just for a good cause. And that's about all you can offer. And as for making a reputation, that's not for me neither. That's just a good way of asking for trouble. And if that means we got trouble here and now, then that's just how it's got to be."

Robles glanced at his men and turned back to the

ex-range detectives, seeing his last reasonable hope drift away. "And you?" he said to Phin.

"I see it like Cajun."

"Then that settles it. As for now, you won't be getting any trouble from us. The decision was yours. I only ask you one thing. Now that you are free to go your own way, I must ask you to give your word not to hire out to Johnny Baehma."

Cajun smiled wryly. "Not much chance of that, even if I wanted to. And I don't." He stepped over to his black. "I was on my way to Red Rock when I first came across Sloan. I didn't like it then and I like it less now. It's about time I get back northward, just as soon as I take care of some personal business."

He saddled up and looked to his side to see Phin following his example. Phin said, "If it's Tolfane you're talking about, it's my business too."

The Mexicans watched the two men ride off in silence. When he finally spoke, Robles' voice was a monotone.

"We forget the cattle. We're going to make our fight."

The other men looked at him incredulously. Even Fernando was too surprised to look pleased.

"If Tolfane has made a deal with Baehma," Robles continued, "then things will get much worse before they get better. Our only chance is now. Camilo, Fernando—go to the other ranches and see whom you can round up."

20

Only three of the ranch hands were about, tending to their usual chores for the day. The rest had apparently joined the detectives in the tracking. The family buckboard stood horseless by the stable. In this picture of quiet orderliness, it was clear that news of the failed assassination had not reached the Tolfane ranch.

Cajun and Phin approached from the east, coming down out of the Huecas a couple of miles away from the ranch house and shielding themselves with the stable to their front. Tolfane made a habit of spending his days in his study where he attended to his paperwork. That room was on the western end of the ground floor. Passing the stable, the two riders casually greeted one of the hands and kept their eyes on the eastern windows as they walked their horses to the house. They saw no movement inside and went on the dismount at the edge of the porch.

Cajun said, "I'm going inside. You stay out here."

"And cheat me out of seeing him sweat?"

"No argument. You've got to keep out anyone who might help him."

Resigned, Phin looked off toward the corrals, slapping the reins in his hand. Cajun tied the black to a porch upright.

"Don't worry, Phin. I'll give him your best."

The man in the serape walked around the corner and let himself in through the back door. Inside the foyer, he heard the cook clattering about somewhere nearby. He edged down the hall, placed himself by the kitchen door, and glanced inside to see the cook carrying an armful of dirty pans toward the basin on the far side of the room. He passed the doorway in a quick stride and, turning the next corner, headed for the front of the house. Moving soundlessly down the paneled corridor, he came to the staircase by the main entrance where he stopped to listen. From upstairs came light footfalls and the faint rustle of skirts. The walking then stopped. To the right, through the half-opened doorway, Cajun heard the scratch of pen on paper.

At the door, he saw Tolfane at his desk, his back to the door, for the moment gazing out the window before him. The rancher set the pen aside and rested his forehead on his laced fingertips. Cajun's voice was a sudden piercing rasp.

"All right you fine-haired son of a bitch, turn around slow."

Tolfane sat absolutely motionless; then, gripping the armrest with a white hand, he swiveled gradually around. The black eyes glazed when he saw Cajun just inside the room, silently closing the door behind him.

"Push the chair away from the desk. Keep your hands still."

The rancher did as he was told. Deliberately crossing the room, Cajun reached into the cabinet on the wall near the desk and took out the bottle of brandy.

177

"You were losing interest in your work, I see. What's the matter? Something on your mind?"

Tolfane sat speechlessly, becoming pale around the mouth and eyes. Cajun uncorked the bottle, took a swig and placed it back on its shelf. The liquor did nothing for the taste in his mouth, something acrid and spreading.

"Talk, Tolfane. Why'd you set us up?"

The rancher struggled for his voice. "Listen, Cajun, I—I was forced into it. I didn't have any choice—"

"Stop the stalling, Tolfane, because that's all you're doing. You're the biggest rancher around here and you weren't forced into shit. So don't try playing for time because Phin's still around too and he's making sure I get all the time I need. Now get started."

Tolfane dropped his head and hunched over, breathing in shallow, audible breaths. After several moments, he began. He told Cajun about his previous arrangement with Baehma and how they'd had their falling out. He explained that his law-and-order stance had just been a front for forcing the outlaws to keep up their end of the old bargain, and that he had used restraint at first because he thought that an early reasonable agreement could be reached. Instead, a desperate one had been arrived at the night before, with Cajun's death a part of it.

Cajun considered the trembling man with penetrating gray eyes made caustic by the lowered, bunched brow. "Okay," he let out through tightened lips, "that explains what you did to me. What about Phin? Baehma didn't care about him."

"That was my idea. He knew too much." His gaze suddenly lifted to meet Cajun's. "We got a deal to make, you and me." His voice took on a desperate resiliency. "It would be worth your while, Cajun. I promise." He grabbed the other man's arm. Cajun threw the hold.

A principal reason for his wanting to talk to Tolfane had been to find out what Phin was involved in, but now that curiosity was swept away. "I've had enough of you," he snarled. "I'm not going to be in the same room with you more than I have to."

"Don't kill me, Cajun! Please, listen! What Phin knew was enough to kill over. It's got to be worth it to you."

Cajun swept his Colt from its holster and held it cocked to Tolfane's face. "I've had enough. You got a choice. Stand up, sit down, or turn around—but you're going to die and that's flat."

"Listen, Cajun. It's the silver. I know where it is."

Both men poised stock-still. Cajun stared at the aristocratic face now pinched with pleading. The rage still ran through him but it was being diffused by a cooler sense. The room stayed soundless for a time that was hard to measure. Then Cajun spat out the words, the anger directed at himself as much as at Tolfane.

"Okay, talk. Make it fast."

The rancher collected himself. "I always knew Johnny would hit some big stake from time to time. When this fighting started between us, I decided the next time he came upon some big cache I would make it my business to find out where he kept it. I wasn't thinking that I'd take it away from him. I was just planning on using the information as a sort of lever against him, maybe to help me win the fight or maybe even afterwards. I needed some kind of insurance against him trying to cut me out again and if I could threaten to tell his men about the loot or tell anyone else who could do something about it, then he might think twice before trying anything with me."

"You said Phin knew something. What was it?"

"I'll tell you. Let me explain. I needed someone to do the dirty work for me. That person was Phin."

"He was looking for the silver because you told him to do it?"

"Not exactly."

"Come on. Out with it."

"I couldn't trust him just like that. You see, how was I to know that as soon as he found out, he wouldn't just go for it himself and leave the territory? I needed something to hold him with. So I used my wife. She's used to that kind of flirting and when Phin responded to her we knew our man. He was supposed to find the silver and then run off with Alicia. That's what he thought. But I knew that this way he would tell my wife where it was hidden and then not do anything about it till she said she was ready." A hint of pride came to his voice through the fear. "I knew he wouldn't tell me where it really was when it was time for him to report to me. In fact, he didn't. But Alicia has told me."

Cajun's questions about Phin's behavior were now answered. Behind it all was plain jealousy. He shifted the weight of the Colt in his hand. "So now I know what was behind it. Now, where's the silver

180

stashed?''

Tolfane's eyes fixed on the muzzle of the gun. "Do we have a deal, for my life?''

"You don't deserve it.''

"It's 20,000 dollars, Cajun! Yours for the taking! If I had that kind of money with me, I'd give it to you.''

Cajun blinked in consternation. A grimace slowly came to his face. A moment later he released the hammer and holstered the gun. "It'll be the death of me yet, I swear.''

On leaving the house, Cajun heard Mrs. Tolfane moving about upstairs once again and considered what Phin would do when he heard what the set-up had been. Cajun would have to clear the air right away. He wasn't about to be tied to any brutality against a wealthy rancher's wife. Regardless of what he thought of her part in it, he wouldn't allow himself to become the prey for the relentless sort of posse that grew out of such a hated crime.

Outside, he walked to his horse, got on top and looked down at Phin without saying a word.

"What went on?'' Phin said. "What'd you do?''

"I made a deal with him.''

"You what? You let the son of a bitch weasel out of it?''

"I'm going to let you know all he told me, but I'm going to get this out right at the start. You been making plans about Mrs. Tolfane—but all the time she was pulling you around to help out her old man!''

"What the hell you sayin'?''

"She was using you to help them find the silver and then Tolfane handed you over to Baehma because you already did everything he wanted you to do.''

Phin's face was red with wild anger, the curl to his lip more arched than usual. "You better not be lying about a thing like that."

"You can be damn sure I'm not."

Phin steamed for a short time, then wheeled towards the house. He stopped when he heard the hammer cock behind him. With gun outstretched, Cajun said, "You're not going anywhere except on that horse and out of here with me." Phin turned to him glaring. Cajun went on.

"I know the silver's in the hideaway under the floor of the old sheriff's office. I ought to shoot you where you stand for not telling me about it. You understand, partner?"

Phin had no answer.

"This is the way it's going to be. Like I said, I've got a right to do just about anything I want to you, but I'm going to give you a chance. And it's a sight better chance than you gave me. You can go for the door and try your luck with me, or we ride out of here and get that loot. I'll still let you have half because I may need some help along the way. What is it going to be? Is she worth 10,000 dollars?"

The other man continued to brood, the muscles tightening along his jaw.

"You going to face the fact that she twisted you in circles or are you going to let her cheat you twice?"

Phin strode to the chestnut and swung into the saddle. "Let's get rich, Cajun."

They took off southward at a lope. The prospect of leaving the area filled Cajun with a surge of energy. A place like Red Rock would be just the spot for a great wad of money. In a town like that a big stake could grow to all sizes and, if it didn't, he would have himself a time losing it.

Nearing the mountains, he slowed briefly, passing the wooden board marker crudely inscribed with the name Lafe Jenkins. He remembered his promise to Lafe about footing the bill for a spree when their job was done. Bitterly, he realized that he would be leaving a job of his own undone.

The two men traveled at a good clip without pressing. By mid-afternoon they came within sight of Sloan. They turned right and picked out a path that would take them to the rear of the sheriff's office. Passing through a small grouping of hillocks, Cajun heard a scraping of a boot heel to the side. He turned quickly toward a greasewood-covered knoll on the right. Coming to the crest from the other side were two Mexicans. As one, Cajun and Phin swung around to the mound behind them when the voice called out.

"I see you have business in town."

Robles came down off the mound and walked towards them, carrying a rifle. "If you are not with us, we must ask you to stay back until after we have settled our own affairs."

21

When the others came into view, Cajun and Phin saw that it was the same six men who had been at Sandoval Ravine earlier in the day. Robles stopped alongside Cajun's black, hefting his Henry to the crook of his arm.

"Have you reconsidered our offer?"

"Not exactly. What's to keep us from going into town now?"

"Baehma and his men are there. We're going in to make our play. We can't have you in town to put them on their guard."

Cajun and Phin exchanged uncertain looks. Turning back to the jefe, Cajun said, "How many are there?"

"All of them. Nine altogether. Two new men came along with Baehma around an hour ago. They've all gone to the cantina for some kind of meeting."

Phin motioned to the men around him. "These are all the men you could get?"

"We tried for more but the rest are scared."

"They've got you outnumbered by three," said Cajun. "How do you expect to take them?"

"We've got surprise on our side. We'll have to make the best of it."

"This is crazy—you know that, don't you?

What're you walking into it for?''

"We have no choice. I told you the others are scared. If we wait anymore there will be even less of us to fight. We may not win, but if we do nothing, we won't be able to live around here anyway. They'll have us under their heel and none of us are willing to live like that.''

"You're probably going to die. What sort of living do you call that?''

"We have worked hard for our homes. This is our only chance to keep them.''

Phin said, "You could at least wait till there are less of them—''

Cajun put a hand on his arm and shook his head to tell him to hold off.

"The two us got some talking to do," he said to Robles. "We'll be right back.''

Cajun and Phin walked their horses off a few yards and glanced back at the Mexicans. The man in the serape leaned toward his partner.

"They're set on it, that's for sure.''

"What can we do?''

"I'm not sure.''

"We can't just stand around, right?''

"No, we can't. They go in and shoot it out, there's a chance things might get desperate and Baehma could run out with the silver to hide it someplace else. Could be someone else might find it. There's not that many places to use for cover there.''

"Seems like we got to keep ourselves close to it.''

Cajun looked off absently. One consideration stood out in front of all others for the moment. Johnny Baehma was a minute's ride away.

He was drawn back by the sudden commotion

185

behind him. The Mexicans were quickly bringing their horses around and mounting up. He and Phin moved back to the group and, looking past the hillock toward town, saw the cause of the activity. Three of the Sloan bunch had left the cantina at the far end of the road and were getting their mounts from the corral in back. Two more came out to join them.

Robles reined his pinto over to the two Anglos. "We go now. You can stay here if you want."

Cajun turned toward town, then back to meet the jefe's gaze. "If it's all the same to you, I'd like to throw in with you."

Robles' eyes shone and the slightest smile came to his lips. As Cajun took his second Colt from his saddle bag, Phin pulled out his carbine. He said, "Looks like you got yourself a couple of 10,000 dollar fighters for only 100 dollars."

The Mexican looked at him quizzically for only a beat, then swung around and prodded his horse forward to lead his troop into town.

Baehma and Josh Claibourne finished their round with the two men from San Miguel and were headed for the door when a shout came from outside.

"Johnny! They're comin' in!"

Baehma rushed to the front door to look down the street. The riders were nearing the shack, coming fast. Ave ran up to him from behind.

"It's the Mexes. They got the Cajun with them. Phin also."

Sol Claibourne and Morgan Fleet came around the other side of the cantina and into the road, their rifles in hand. Baehma pulled one of his

186

Smith & Wessons and faced the group as Amos and Tobey joined the others. The riders had now reached the shack. The outlaw chief turned to the two newcomers, Penrose and Selman.

"You come with me. Ave too. We'll take the other side of the street. Everyone spread. Move!"

Baehma and the three others ran across the road. Josh, Sol, and Tobey took cover around the cantina. Fleet and Amos started for the abandoned signmaker's shop. Gunfire erupted from all sides.

The horse under Lucero went down, sending the man tumbling. Another slug crippled Urbina's animal and he also ended in the dirt. Most of the Mexicans circled back around the shack. They passed Fleet and Amos running in the other direction and broke into a small skirmish.

Cajun and Phin swung wide and came to a jolting stop behind the provision store. Jumping from their saddles, they took position at opposite corners and levered their rifles at the figures darting behind the sheriff's office. Fernando rode in the their rear. Urbina scrambled toward the store, then jerked into a back rending arch, froze for a moment, and collapsed to the ground.

Fernando rode hard out into the road. As he approached the wounded man, Josh and Tobey opened up on him. Cajun rattled off the rest of his magazine, giving them some trouble. Urbina was able to push himself up and grab the lowered arm. Fernando half-carried, half-dragged him back to the store while a volley of fire from the Mexicans at the shack kept down the outlaws by the cantina.

From the sheriff's office, Penrose and Ave took off for a mound away from the road. Taking the saddle bags off his black to get more cartridge tubes, Cajun was by the back of the store and could see them make their move. As Phin chased them with rifle fire, Cajun saw that the next form of cover leading to the store was a hollow ten feet further on from the mound. He slipped in the new tube, hurried for the front of the building, and passed across its entrance to the corner opposite the sheriff's office.

The outlaws had reached the protection of the mound. Cajun waited with his back flush against the wall. A moment later, Ave and Penrose charged out for the hollow. Cajun pivoted around the corner and flicked off two shots almost as one. The man from San Miguel pitched forward in a tangled sprawl. Ave leaped and rolled to his cover underneath the fire. Across the way, the Smith & Wesson spoke in a cluster of three, forcing Cajun back to the recessed doorway.

Baehma bounded forward over the razed wall and into the rubble, keeping up the pressure. Exposed to the other side of road, Cajun faced more fire coming from Fleet and Amos by the signmaker shop. Chips of wood from the door spattered onto his face. He heaved against the door, forced it open, and lunged inside away from the hail of bullets.

Seizing the moment, Morgan Fleet rushed forward, pumping lead at the shack as he went, getting cover fire from Amos. Peering through the open doorway, Cajun saw Fleet about to cross the road and drew a bead. Baehma's fire from the side made him shift his position and hurry his shots. He missed. He rolled to the other side of the opening to angle himself for a shot at Fleet reaching the near side, but some new fast shooting sent him a foot further and the extra movement cost him. Fleet reached the sheriff's office and Cajun's shot whistled through empty air.

Cajun sneaked a look across the road to see where the unexpected firing had come from. At the well between the cantina and the shack was Josh, who had stolen over from the south end of the street. From the cantina, Sol followed his brother, dashing across the open toward the well. Stretched across the floor, Cajun lined up the Spencer, judged the man's speed, and triggered. Nothing. He tossed the empty rifle aside and rolled over, grabbing for his Colt, seeing the man approach his cover. Before he had the handgun leveled, he heard the crack from the north side of the store and saw Sol drop. Phin had been watching too.

Baehma sent Selman out to back up Ave, who was trading shots with Fernando by the store. The new man made it to the protection of the mound while, side by side, Fleet and the outlaw chief kept Cajun and Phin low.

"Stay here," Baehma said, straining to be heard over the constant barrage. "I'm going to try the back." He turned and, running in a crouch, reached the low point in the back wall and rolled over it. He ejected his shells and started reloading to find Fleet dropping down beside him.

"I told you to stay there."

"I know." Fleet sent a couple of shots toward the back of the store. "I just thought I'd stick with ya."

"What the hell for?"

"Want to make sure you live. And if you leave in a hurry, I want to be there."

Baehma glared at him suspiciously, but dismissed it as he put in his last cartridge.

The fighting at the north end of the road intensified, the bellowing of guns becoming an almost continuous roar. The Mexicans, now split on either side of the pinewood shack, kept Josh pinned down behind the well and Amos to the rear of the signmaker shop. Tobey tried making it to Josh's side but couldn't get past the corner of the cantina. Tomas' brother, Joachim, tried rushing the shop. He was just past halfway there when he was cut down by Josh. In the moment when Claibourne got off the shot with his shoulders up into the clear, a bullet from Robles' Henry flattened him to the ground with a neat blue hole in his skull.

Cajun went to a store window in the south wall, cracked out a corner of the glass, and snapped a few shots at the back of the sheriff's office. Baehma and Fleet backed off under the flurry. With pressure eased from the other side of the street, Phin came around to the front of the store and started on them from that angle.

Fleet leaned over so Baehma could hear. "They've got three of us already. What's it gonna be, Johnny?"

The outlaw chief ducked under a glancing shot and turned to his man irritably. He took in Fleet's foxy look and realized that his suspicions of a minute ago were correct. Morgan was the back-trailer.

Fleet said, "I was up there this morning. Saw that you took it away."

They returned fire, and then Baehma came up with an answer. "You and me—we'll get outa here."

"I'm right with you."

At the far corner of the store, Baehma caught sight of Fernando taking an extra step toward the open for a shot at Ave. A Smith & Wesson jumped up and rang out twice. The Mexican spun back behind the corner. The bottom of his legs could still be seen along the ground. They dragged slowly toward cover, then stopped.

Baehma turned back to Fleet. There was only one place he wanted to be now. He said, "I'm going toward the front. You work around the back. We'll meet by the horses."

Without waiting for an answer, he went over the wall, back into the rubble. By the front left corner, he fired out of a window toward Phin, turning away at the sound of the voice to his side.

"That's not close enough," Fleet said, crouched inside the ruined office. "You're not getting away from me." He crawled over to the outlaw chief and grabbed his arm. "This is how it'll be. You and—"

Baehma threw him off with a powerful shrug, nearly thrusting him up to his feet.

From the window in the store, Cajun could see Fleet's head bob up above the jagged half-wall of the law office. Next he saw two shoulders struggling against each other for another moment. Then Fleet was hit hard and he passed into view from the waist up. The black Colt fired and Fleet was flung aside with the force of the slug. The near wall in the office was splattered with the blood jetting from his neck.

Squatting on the other side, Baehma started at Fleet's motionless body, only momentarily surprised. He took stock of his situation. Four dead now. Only four others left beside himself. They could be enough of a distraction if he wanted to

191

play it that way.

He reached down and swung open the hideaway door. He dragged the sack up, feeling its reassuring heft and judging his chances of carrying it to his horse. After all, he didn't owe the four men anything, living or dead.

Cajun tired of the stalemate. He knew Baehma was behind that wall and he could guess what he was thinking. He filled his loads, went to the door, came up behind Phin and said, "I'm going for him."

He raced diagonally across toward the back of the sheriff's office, firing on the run. Baehma got off a wild shot, then held off. Cajun dove for the protection of the rear wall, came up to a crouch, moved on several yards and swung his right arm over the top of the wall, emptying his chambers.

Scrambling to a charred, overturned desk, Baehma fired back twice and then stayed low until Cajun dropped down.

The Louisiana man would have his fight all right —as soon as the outlaw chief got himself out of the corner. He shot once at Phin, and once at Cajun, then bolted through the front door and across the road. Cajun vaulted over the wall and crossed over to the side of the door to see the outlaw making it to the far side of the cantina.

Ejecting his shells and reloading, he glanced back at the corner and saw the sack lying there for the taking. He thumbed in his fifth cartridge, snapped shut the cylinder, and let the silver lie, charging out and shooting his way to the other side of the street.

22

The fighting continued in a semi-circular sweep around the two men poised on opposite sides of the cantina. Amos and Tobey found themselves outnumbered by one and badly positioned. They started working their way back to the south end of the road, angling for the corral and their horses. Ave and Selman could see what their cronies were up to from their side. That and the fact that Johnny had moved off gave them doubts, even though only one healthy man was shooting at them. They also started edging away, toward the two horses tied to the post some twenty yards behind the sheriff's office.

Cajun stopped after a few paces, leaned back against the wall with his Colt leveled, concentrating his hearing, trying to filter any sound from the other side of the cantina through the bark of gunfire around him. In a fleeting gap in the shooting, he heard the faint crunch of boot heel against earth. Taking a chance on an instinctive impression, he judged that it came from further back. The last he'd been aware of Baehma, the outlaw had been near the front corner. Stealing back in a crouch, Cajun moved as fast as he dared to the rear corner. He braced himself with one eye lined along the back wall, frozen in place. After a moment that brought sweat around his eyes, he saw a leg inch beyond the opposite corner. When a thin line of torso came into view, he squeezed the trigger. The shot was wide and before he could get off another a .44 slug plowed across the adobe wall less than a foot away from him. Cajun spun away toward the front.

He waited for the other man's move but couldn't detect any. He hated himself for having wasted the shot, but, more than that, he was struck by how fast Baehma got off his own, and how close it was.

Not hearing anything around the back, he started forward. The gunfire across the street thickened.

Ave and Selman, reaching the edge of their respective covers, came to their feet at the same time and fired rapidly at Phin's position. They then wheeled and took off at a dead run for the horses. Phin came out after them. Once he was well out into the open, he saw both of them turn to fire. He rushed for the mound ten yards away. He got off a shot and on the next stride dove for the cover. He flinched in mid-air as something hot bore into his groin. He thudded down behind the mound with a sickening groan. The wounded Urbina managed to keep up some sporadic fire with his rifle from the other end of the store and the two outlaws had to slow down.

Cajun approached the cantina's side window, sidling up alongside it. He turned slowly to steal a look inside and across at the window in the opposite wall. At the reverberating blast he dropped suddenly for protection, the pane smashing above him. From the other side, Baehma had beat him to the trick, shooting across the room. Swiveling up to a crouch, Cajun saw the two figures out of the edge of his eye. Amos and Tobey had shot their way to the corral, some fifty feet away. As Cajun noticed them, Amos swung his rifle around to cut loose. Partially turned away from the corral and in no position to beat him to the shot, Cajun was forced to flatten under the fire and then scramble up toward the front corner.

He fired back twice on the run, knowing he was using up his last load, not knowing what he'd find around the corner. While moving, he shifted the spent Colt to his left hand and grabbed for the gun in his belt with his right. As he reached for the weapon, a rifle slug tore through his left side, tugging him down. He was able to twist to the left as he fell and flop to the ground just behind the cover of the corner. But he hit the dirt with his right hand empty. The gun had flipped away from him upon impact and now lay five feet away.

The firing from the corral stopped and Cajun could make out the heavy running fall of boots. Baehma was coming. With his side throbbing in pain, Cajun clawed, dragged, and pushed himself along the ground toward the gun. Coming within reach, his thinking knotted as he realized what hadn't occurred to him before. He had been so absorbed in the pain of his wound that he hadn't noticed the way the gun lay. It was at a forty-five degree angle, butt forward and facing away to the left. An easy grab for the left hand—but for the right a clumsy, crucially time-wasting effort. He heard the footfalls approach the front corner and, in a transfixed instant, he took in the possibilities and saw his play. A border roll.

As Baehma charged into view, Cajun lunged for

the gun, clawing his hand over it and curling his finger around the trigger guard, in a single motion, he spun it around, slapped the handle into his palm, cocked the hammer, and fired. Baehma's Smith & Wesson went off convulsively as the .45 slug caught him in the middle of his chest and exited behind, taking a part of his back with it. The thick body teetered briefly, then fell back stiffly and hit the ground like a sack of stone.

Cajun forced himself to his knees, his Colt still trained, and held himself poised for a short time. He let the gun arm sag. The man was already dead.

Hoof beats came from the corral and, struggling to his feet, Cajun lurched for the side of the cantina and worked his way to the rear. Tobey was riding off away from the town, to the east. In the other direction, Amos drummed across the other side of the adobe toward the street. Cajun took aim at Tobey's receding figure but figured he was out of range.

He examined his bleeding side. It would give him problems for awhile but wouldn't be too serious. The bullet had passed through the fleshy part just above the hip and hadn't hit anything vital. The pain soon gave way to something else in his consciousness. There was just one thing left to do before leaving Sloan.

Walking slowly to the street, he saw that the two outlaws on the other side had also made off, having finally reached the horses at the post. Occasional gunfire was directed at the distant horsemen, but the impression of sudden relative quiet in the town was undisturbed. Robles and Tomas came up to Cajun in the road, asking how he was and congratulating him on his fight with Johnny

Baehma. Cajun answered curtly and was relieved when they left him to see to Phin and Urbina by the store. He hobbled up to the old sheriff's office, rounded the single intact side, stepped over the low wall, and stopped short.

The sack was gone.

Cajun prodded himself over to the corner where he had seen it before, began thrashing through the debris, and then, swerving toward the northwest, locked his eyes on something in the distance. It was Amos Claibourne. Cajun suddenly remembered the angle of the man's ride from the corral toward the other side of the road. Straining his eyes for the distance, he now thought he could see an extra bulge across the saddle.

Robles and Tomas found Phin behind the mound, bleeding badly. The jefe sent the boy off to get the bandages in his kit and knelt beside him.

"We'll take care of you," Robles said. "After what you and your friend have done, it is the least we can do."

Phin was able to speak with effort. "They've gone off?"

"Yes, they have. Those that could. Your friend killed Johnny Baehma. With him gone, chances are the others won't bother coming back."

Phin nodded weakly.

"Anything you and your friend want, we'll give you, the best we can. You are big men now. I think we will remember this day for a long time."

Phin's eyes slowly took on a sharpened glint as he remembered his reasons for being here this day. With a wince, he raised his head. "The Cajun. Where is he? Is he here?"

"Why, yes. I just left him in the road. He's been

197

hit but I think he'll be all right.''

The Mexican scanned the road, looking for the man. At the fast clatter of hoofs, he snapped his head around, toward the north end of town. Cajun Lee was galloping out from behind the store, swinging in a wide curve and taking off for the northwest. Robles watched without speaking as the man sped toward the horizon, hunched over to the left side, willing himself to stay in the saddle.

Epilogue

On the twenty-first of December, 1879, the town of Silverton, Colorado was shocked at the violent death of one of its most respected citizens. The story was reported the next day in The Silverton Nugget.

MURDER

Reverend Killed At Home

Culprit Not Found

On Wednesday evening, about 11 o'clock, the Reverend Amos T. Johnson was murdered in his home by an unidentified assailant. He was found in the drawing room of his two-story house at the south end of town minutes after the act was committed. He was shot in the chest and abdomen and was holding a pistol in his hand, apparently attempting to defend his home against the intruder. The safe at the rear of the house was broken into and its contents taken.

The town was immediately searched after the discovery, but the murderer could not be found. Suspicions, however, are rife. Most notable of these concerns a stranger who remains nameless and is identified only by the black serape he wore throughout his short visit to our town. He arrived in Silverton three days ago and is said to have left immediately after the killing.

Reverend Johnson was one of our most successful and admired citizens and his death has caused great mourning in Silverton. Since coming here two months ago, his sermons and good works have been an inspiration to many and, in his honor, business houses were draped in black on Thursday.

Lawlessness of this sort has touched many of our citizens' lives of late and the time has come for a firm hand to be taken. What is called for is the kind of resolute action that so dramatically rid southern New Mexico of the terrible Claibourne-Laughlin gang. If the law is helpless, the time has come for private citizens to do what they can.

GUN TROUBLE IN TONTO BASIN

ROMER ZANE GREY

Gun Trouble In Tonto Basin signals the reappearance of Arizona Ames, the title character of one of Zane Grey's most memorable novels. Young Rich Ames came to lead the life of a range drifter after he participated in a gunfight that left two men dead. Ames' skill earned him a reputation as one of the fastest guns in the West.

In these splendid stories, Arizona Ames comes home to find his range and his family haunted by the shadow of a terror they dare not name!

WESTERN
0-8439-2098-X
$2.75

THE OTHER SIDE OF THE CANYON

ROMER ZANE GREY

THE OTHER SIDE OF THE CANYON marks the return to print of one of Zane Grey's strongest characters, Laramie Nelson, first introduced in Grey's novel RAIDERS OF SPANISH PEAKS. Laramie was a seasoned Indian fighter, an incomparable tracker, and one of the deadliest gunhands the West had ever known.

In these stories, Romer Zane Grey, son of the master storyteller, continues Laramie's adventures as he takes on a gang of train robbers, a gold thief, and a sharp-shooting woman wanted for murder!

WESTERN
8439
2041-6
$2.75

THE RIDER OF DISTANT TRAILS

ROMER ZANE GREY

The Rider Of Distant Trails marks the return to print of one of Zane Grey's most memorable characters, Buck Duane, first introduced in Grey's novel *Lone Star Ranger*. Forced to turn outlaw as a young man, Buck later teamed up with Captain Jim MacNelly of the Texas Rangers and proved himself to be the Ranger's deadliest gun.

In these stories, Romer Zane Grey, son of the master storyteller, continues Buck's adventures in Texas and as he takes on outlaws who are terrorizing ranches and towns in this tough cattle country!

WESTERN
0-8439-2082-3
$2.75

Make the Most of Your Leisure Time
with
LEISURE BOOKS

Please send me the following titles:

Quantity	Book Number	Price
_____	_____	_____
_____	_____	_____
_____	_____	_____
_____	_____	_____
_____	_____	_____

If out of stock on any of the above titles, please send me the alternate title(s) listed below:

_____	_____	_____
_____	_____	_____
_____	_____	_____
_____	_____	_____

	Postage & Handling	_____
	Total Enclosed	$_____

☐ Please send me a free catalog.

NAME _____
(please print)

ADDRESS _____

CITY _____ STATE _____ ZIP _____

Please include $1.00 shipping and handling for the first book ordered and 25¢ for each book thereafter in the same order. All orders are shipped within approximately 4 weeks via postal service book rate. PAYMENT MUST ACCOMPANY ALL ORDERS.*

*Canadian orders must be paid in US dollars payable through a New York banking facility.

Mail coupon to: **Dorchester Publishing Co., Inc.**
6 East 39 Street, Suite 900
New York, NY 10016
Att: ORDER DEPT.